RUIN

The Complete Series

New York Times & USA Today Bestselling Author
Deborah Bladon

Copyright

First Original Edition, November 2014
Copyright © 2014 by Deborah Bladon
ISBN-13: 978-1505214475
ISBN-10: 1505214475

Cover Design by Wolf & Eagle Media.

Also by Deborah Bladon

The Obsessed Series
The Exposed Series
The Pulse Series
The VAIN Series
IMPULSE
SOLO

Coming Soon

FUSE
The GONE Series

RUIN

Part One

Chapter 1

"I keep a room at a hotel in mid-town. We can go there."

The words are decisive and seductive. The subtle hum of his voice catering to the need that is inside of me. The same need that drove me away from Boston and back into the uneven clutches of Manhattan.

I glance at my watch. Fifty-nine minutes. It's been fifty-nine minutes since he sat next to me on this flight. Thirty-one minutes since he told me he's always been attracted to brunettes. Twenty-five minutes since I knew that having his cock inside of me would chase away all the deepest memories of the man I left behind.

"I have a driver meeting me." The assumption is there. He's moved effortlessly from asking if I'm interested to expecting it. He knows how utterly attractive he is. The eager glances of the flight attendant who tried to divert his attention from me spoke of the pull that is there within him, whether he's consciously sending out signals or not.

I nod. It's not unlike me. He's not the first man I've slept with within moments of meeting. It's always filled a temporary hunger. This time is different though. This time I'm doing it to numb the ache.

"I'm Ben, by the way." He extends his hand in a graceful, yet misplaced, greeting.

I reach for it, entrusting my own in his. "I'm Kayla."

"Pretty," he says.

I take the compliment along with the gentle touch. He won't be like this in bed. I can sense it already. There's a darkness behind his eyes that promises skill, pleasure and a bite of flashing pain. It's everything I need all wrapped into a six foot four inch, muscular, brown haired, brown eyed stranger.

"Is anyone expecting you?"

My eyes flit across his face pulling nothing from his stoic expression. He's asking if there's a complication waiting for me when the plane touches down at LaGuardia. There's nothing waiting for me here. No one knows that I've run from my life in Boston. I haven't told a soul that the man I loved left me beneath the shadow of an excuse about chasing his own happiness. He'd changed overnight. The once beautiful, confident soul that held me in his arms and promised me a lifetime has been replaced with a cold, distant selfish asshole.

"No," I whisper the word as if that will lessen the pain that is attached to it. "There's no one."

"I need to make a few calls once we land." His hand dives into an inner pocket of his Armani suit jacket to retrieve his smart phone. "I'll do that while you grab your luggage."

I pull my hands over the smooth denim of my worn jeans. I look ordinary next to him. I'll disappear into the crowds of the airport the moment we depart from the plane. He'll command the attention of many. He wants that. It's part of who he is.

"I don't have any checked bags," I begin before I realize the words sound comfortable and intimate in a way that I don't want them to. "I'll wait outside for you."

He flashes a grin. "You won't run away on me?"

I'm not Parker. Parker, my piece of shit boyfriend, ran away on me. He told me he loved me. He promised me forever and then he ran away.

"I promise I won't." I exhale. "I'll be right there waiting for you."

***

"Your cunt is as beautiful as the rest of you." His breath whispers over my folds before his tongue pierces into me again.

I lean back into the coarse linens that line the bed, throwing my head back. "Make me come again."

He laps at me, his fingers probing my inner walls before he hones in on the spot that he knows will throw me into the middle of another powerful orgasm. My hands reach for his hair. I wind my fingers into the strands, reveling in the softness. I twist his head sharply to the left coaxing his tongue back to my clit. I'm not going to be shy. There's no reason not to take everything I can from this. He's eager to please. I'm eager to come.

"Christ, you're a tight one."

The words only spur me on more. This is exactly what I need. "Lick my clit," I bite out through a moan. "Lick my fucking clit."

He cups his hands beneath my legs pulling them farther apart before they seek out my breasts. He pinches both nipples in unison as his tongue greedily steals another climax from me.

I scream, not only from the intense pleasure that is racing through each part of me, but from the freedom to feel this deeply. I cling to his hair as he moans into me, lapping greedily at my lust.

"I'm so hard. I have to fuck you." The words aren't tempered. They escape him in a growl that is primitive and speaks of his need to own my body.

I watch as he sheaths his thick cock in a condom, his hand racing over the length not once, but twice. I whimper knowing that it's going to throw me back into an orgasm quickly. I've been imagining it since he lowered himself into the seat next to me on the airplane. I've been thinking about how it will feel since I watched him slowly undress when we got to the room. I've been craving it since his erection brushed against my pussy before he lowered his face to my core.

His mouth covers mine as he edges the tip of his dick over my clit. His lips are smooth, soft and gentle. His tongue glides onto mine as he thrusts his cock into me in one fluid, lust filled violent movement. His rhythm is smooth, confident and controlled.

"Yes," I mutter beneath my breath and into his mouth because my body offers no other choice. I need to express it. I need to feel it.

His hands leap to mine, pushing them into the mattress. "Your cunt is so ready."

My body responds and I'm driven over the edge into an orgasm that grips both of us.

"Fuck, Kayla." His words fall into the air between us. "Kayla, yes."

I arch my back, clench my muscles and sigh as he pumps himself into me over and over, each thrust deeper than the last until he finds his release with my name pouring from his lips.

Chapter 2

"Get on your knees."

I stop. The hot water beating a path down my breasts before it skims over my stomach. I'd slept for hours after he left. He told me the room was mine until noon when the housekeeping staff would arrive. I needed the time. I needed the space and the empty air to think. I'd woken shortly after ten, my body aching from last night. The shower was my last reprieve before I had to face the world, my best friend, and the truth about what had chased me out of Boston.

"You came back." The words are foolish and unnecessary.

"On your knees, Kayla," he says against my shoulder before his lips blaze a path up my neck. "You're going to suck my cock."

My sex aches at the demand. It was my only regret as he walked out the door. "Yes," I whisper as his lips graze over mine.

"I've thought about your beautiful mouth since I fucked you last night."

I move closer to him feeling the unmistakable brush of his cock against my stomach. He reaches for my hand, a gesture that speaks of well-mannered courtesy as I lower myself to my knees.

"I've never seen eyes as blue as yours." His hand slides over my chin. "Look at me when you suck it."

I nod as I grab the thick root with my hand. My lips open slightly kissing the very tip. The head is wide, spongy and gorgeous. I pull my tongue down the length, feeling the vein that is pulsing beneath my touch.

"Take it now. Suck it hard." The words have a firm bite to them. "Look at me, Kayla."

My eyes lock on his as I take his cock into my mouth, swirling my tongue around the tip. I murmur around his flesh as I find my rhythm.

"Goddamn, you know how to suck cock." The words are heavy with desire. "I'm going to fuck your mouth so hard."

The promise is only tempered by the space. He leans back slightly, resting his back against the subway tile that surrounds the bathtub. His hands tangle within the long strands of my dark hair. I murmur slightly at the slight rush of pain when he pulls on it.

"Like that, Kayla," he hisses into the rushing stream of water that is bearing down on my side. "Suck it hard."

I up the tempo, my hand racing seamlessly up and down the length while my head bobs in unison pulling him deeper with each thrust of his hips. He's fucking my mouth hard, the sounds escaping his lips pulling even more desire from me.

"Fuck. Oh fuck. Suck it like that." Each of the words falls into the other between low groans. "Christ, Kayla. I'm going to come."

I pull back slightly as he rams his ass into the tiles trying to dislodge his cock from my mouth. I hold steady, my fists still wrapped tightly around it. I gaze up at him, staring directly into his eyes.

"I'm coming," he hisses loudly. "Coming."

I lick my lips as the first stream hits them. I hold him steady capturing every drop on my tongue and my lips.

"Holy fuck." His eyes bore into me watching every movement I make. "Jesus."

***

"Are you from New York or Boston?" His voice is tranquil now. He's come down from the edge. He's dressed in a different suit than last night. This one is navy blue. The white dress shirt he's wearing unbuttoned enough to show a hint of the smooth skin of his chest.

I debate before I answer. "I'm from Boston," I offer in a low tone.

"You're just visiting here?" He reaches towards the floor. His hand elegantly pulling at the edge of the scarf that I'd dropped when I'd undressed last night.

I take it from him with a slight nod of my head. "I'm moving back here."

"You've lived here before?"

I stare at him unsure of whether he's making small talk to avoid the uncomfortable silence that drifts between two strangers after they've shared an exchange that intimate. "I did, briefly," I whisper into the scarf that I've now pulled around my neck.

His eyes drop from my face to the floor. "I grew up in Boston. I like New York more."

I hate Boston. "I do too, "I say slowly. I will like it more. I have to. I don't want to go back there.

"I'm driving today." His hand dips into the pocket of his pants. I hear the clink of keys as he shuffles them within his palm. "Is there somewhere I can drop you?"

I study his face. The curve of his brow and the strength in his jawline is familiar. I've seen his face before. "Have we met before?"

His brown eyes meet mine. "I would remember meeting you."

"You're sure?" I push back wanting to make the connection. I'd fucked a few boys in college but he's older than me. There's no way he's twenty-three-years-old too. The way he carries himself is different. His clothing suggests he's wealthier than someone who would normally stay in a room like this. The realization of that stings a touch. I instantly wonder if he brings all the women he fucks here or if there's another, more comfortable, place for those he deems worthy.

"We haven't met." His eyes avoid mine. "I have to get to work."

The natural reaction would be to ask where that is. I should want to know how he fills his days and what those perfectly manicured hands do that affords him the expensive watch around his wrist and the silver cufflinks that pop into view every now and again beneath the cuff of his jacket.

I shuffle slightly on my feet, pulling on the hem of the blue sweater I'm wearing. I should thank him. How do I do that? Do I tell him that I appreciate the orgasms? Do I applaud him for gifting me with the talents of his tongue? "Thank you for letting me stay here last night."

"Kayla?" My name falls from his lips in a low rasp. "You have somewhere to go, don't you?"

"Yes." I have a place I can go to. I don't belong anywhere right now.

"You're sure?" Concern blankets over his expression. "You can stay here for a few days if you need to."

Pity. It's there in his eyes. I see it. "I'm sure," I lie. It's not a complete lie. My best friend will take me in. She'll hold me while I cry over Parker's rejection. She'll make me laugh with stories of the moments in college when life felt easy and the future seemed uncomplicated.

"Last night was fun." He stands in place, his back to the door. "I'm glad we met."

I'm glad we fucked.

Those are the words I'm tempted to say. I am glad he took my body and mind to a place where nothing but pleasure mattered for a few moments. I'm grateful that I didn't have to immediately face my life again. The pain that had been biting at my chest since Parker left me is dulled now. I don't want that to be temporary. I want today to be the first day when I don't feel suffocated with sadness.

"I need to go to the …" he stops himself. The details of his life outside the walls of this room don't matter. He knows they don't.

I nod, fishing in my purse for my smartphone. I'm not good at this part. I don't know what to say as we walk away into the world again. Our brief encounter will become a fond memory in weeks and the details will be so muddled in a year that I'll struggle to recall his face. I glance at him again. No, wait. I won't forget that face. He's as handsome as any man you'd see layered in a beautiful suit on the pages of a magazine. His hair is cut short, but it's still long enough that a woman's yearning fingers can get lost in it. His jaw is sharp and bold, yet there's a tenderness woven into his smile that is disarming.

He steps towards me, his hand leaping to cup my cheek. His eyes catch mine in a warm gaze. "You're amazing, Kayla. Truly. Amazing."

My lips part slightly as if I'm going to say something back but the words don't come. I just stare at him wanting to soak in every detail.

He leans down and slides his lips over mine in a tender kiss. "I'll never forget you," he whispers against my lips.

"I'll never forget you," I repeat back into his beautiful mouth. I won't. This is a man no woman could ever forget.

Chapter 3

"You can stay here as long as you want." Alexa reaches to hand me a trio of soft, white towels. "You can use these to have a shower now, and then you'll always find some in the cabinet in your bathroom."

I'm grateful for the hospitality, but more than that I welcome the literal and figurative embrace she's given me since I walked through her door fifteen minutes ago. She wasn't expecting me. Her face was a twisted mix of joy and confusion when I stepped off the elevator and into her arms. Alexa Jackson is one of my closest friends. She knows my heart. She understands the sacrifices I made when I left New York three months ago to go back to Boston.

"Where's Noah?" I ask, not necessarily out of curiosity, as much as greed. I want her all to myself for the day. It's Tuesday, which means she'd normally be at school, teaching her young students about history and science, but it's spring break so her time is mine.

Her face softens. "He's got a few shoots today and then he's meeting his father for a late lunch."

I sigh in relief. Alexa's fiancé is an in demand photographer. Although his core business is now centered on children and infants, he does an occasional spread in a magazine. He's talented, accomplished and very eccentric. My time with him has been limited up to this point but now that I've taken over their guest room, I'll be seeing a lot more of him.

"Do you want to talk about Parker?" The effortless ease with which she says his name tears through me. I haven't been able to utter his name since he walked out of our apartment. I've avoided every image or reminder of him.

I lower myself to the edge of the queen sized bed I'll be calling my refuge until I can sort through my life. "There's not much to talk about."

She settles next to me, her hand reaching for mine. She cradles it gently in her lap. "Is it over?"

I hear the words clearly. I don't react. I just stare at her hand and the large diamond ring that is catching the natural sunlight streaming through the window. She's going to plan her wedding soon. She'll marry the man of her dreams and her life will start on its course towards a happily-ever-after that she rightly deserves. I deserve it too though and now I have to confess that my prince charming pulled the rug out from under me without any warning.

"Did you have a fight?" she presses.

I can't blame her for wanting to know. The last time we spoke was barely more than a week ago when I told her of my plans to visit New York with Parker in tow. I wanted to hold his hand in Central Park and feel his lips brush against mine while we soaked in the view atop the Empire State Building. I wanted his body to give me pleasure in a bed in a decadent hotel on the Upper West Side. I wanted to experience life with him.

I squeeze her hand slightly drawing strength from the familiar touch. "Parker left me." The words float off my tongue and into the stillness of the mid-morning air. "He left me, Alexa."

Her eyes dart to my face and I watch as they race over my features. "No, Kayla. He wouldn't do that."

"He did," I bite back in a tone that speaks of the pain. It's the same overwhelming pain that I've been carrying within me for the past week. "He's gone."

"What happened?"

I draw in a quick breath hoping that it will offer some inspiration. "I don't know. He just said he wasn't happy."

"He wasn't happy with you?"

I nod. I'd replayed Parker's words over and over in my mind since he told me he wanted to find himself and his own happiness. The words were a poorly crafted excuse for him to start fresh without me. They stung just as much as if he would have told me he stopped loving me.

"He begged you to come back to him a few months ago." She holds my hand tighter, squeezing it more. "You left everything here to go be with him."

"I know." I swallow hard. "He told me he couldn't live without me."

Those were the exact words that Parker had muttered through the phone when he'd called me just a few months ago while I was just settling into my life in Manhattan. We'd broken up time and time again after meeting in high school. My heart always knew that we'd find our way back to one another and when he finally called that wintery evening to profess his unwavering devotion, I had packed up everything to be with him. Now, only twelve short weeks later, he was gone and I was back in New York.

"Maybe he was just panicked because he loves you so much."

They're words meant to placate women with broken hearts. The idea behind them is romantic and charming and conjures up an image of a man so overwrought with the knowledge that his heart belongs to a certain woman that he can't bear it. It's not a notion that is seated in any kind of reality. Parker didn't leave me because he loves me. He left me because he's a worthless piece of shit and is too immature to be honest about his feelings.

"It's over, Lex." I pull my hand from hers. "I'm going to put it behind me."

The skepticism floating over her expression isn't masked at all. "You can't just shut off your feelings like that."

She's right. I can't. I can decide to push them aside while I rebuild my life. That needs to be my sole focus right now. If I give in to the overwhelming pain I feel over Parker pushing my life into freefall mode, I'll be paralyzed. I'll hide within myself and I won't move forward. I'm not about to give him that much control over me.

"I need to find a job and a place." A change of subject never hurt anyone. In my case, it may actually dull the pain of talking about Parker.

"You know what they say about break ups, right?" She tilts her head to the side as she pulls a hand through her long blond hair.

"Oh, God." I can't help but chuckle. "Just tell me."

"They say…" she begins before pulling her arm around my shoulder. "They say that you need to date again right away to forget the old love."

"Date?" I shake my head. There's no way in hell I'm dating anytime soon.

"Or fuck," she says with a giggle. "You should find a guy to sleep with. It needs to be someone really hot. If you do that you'll forget about Parker like that." She pulls her fingers together in a snap.

I should tell her. I should tell her about Ben but I stop myself before the words reach my tongue. I want Ben to my secret. I want to hold onto the feeling of being wanted in such a primitive way. I want to hold it close. I want the memory to be mine and only mine.

Chapter 4

"I'm surprised to see you back so soon," Vivian, my former boss, and hopefully soon-to-be present boss, tilts her glasses onto the bridge of her nose as she stares at me.

Hear that noise? That's the sound of me swallowing my pride. Vivian was the one who told me that giving up a promising career, as an account executive at Rainer & Winslow, for a man was a mistake. Good on Vivian for having the foresight to see that my boyfriend was a loser. Not so good on me for not listening to her mini lecture about how he wouldn't sacrifice as much for me. Now, I'm back with my tail between my legs begging for my old position back.

"Things didn't work out in Boston," I say through a thin smile.

She pulls her glasses off completely now. Why do I feel like this is about to get serious? "We've already filled your position, Kayla."

Shit. Shit. Shit.

"I'm not surprised." I am surprised. Vivian isn't the most organized woman on this planet. I'm mildly shocked that she had the wherewithal to screen prospective applicants, interview them and then fill the position. When I worked for her, I was amazed most days when she tore her attention away from the movies she typically had streaming on her computer to give me a task to do.

Her eyes dart to her laptop screen and I wonder briefly if an episode of her favorite detective drama is pulling her attention away. "I need an assistant."

I push myself closer to the edge of the chair I'm sitting in. I need that. I'll take that. I don't care what it pays or what the responsibilities are. "I'd make a great assistant," I say a little too exuberantly.

"You know what?" Her gaze settles back on me. "I think you're right."

My shoulders sway forward. "I'd appreciate the chance to show you what a great asset I can be."

Her face softens as a small smile pulls at the corner of her lips. "You've already done that, Kayla."

I don't want to sound too eager but she's handing me a golden ticket out of Alexa and Noah's guest room. I've only been there five days but I already feel like a third wheel. "When can I start?"

She tips her head back a touch as she pulls her glasses back on. "Monday will be fine. I can pay you the same as what you were getting when you left but the workload will be more."

I know it will be. I'm suddenly aware that it's very likely that I'll not only be shouldering whatever she throws my way but a lot of her work too. Normally, I'd balk at the added responsibility but it's exactly what I need right now. "I'm ready to take on anything."

Her expression shifts slightly as she leans back. "I'm going to hold you to that."

I don't question what she means. I don't care right now. All I know is that this is the first step in getting my life and future back.

***

"Do you think you'll live alone or will you get a roommate?" Alexa's eyes scan the pint sized kitchen of the walk up we're currently touring in Murray Hill.

"If I live here, I can do it alone." I try not to say the words with as much distaste as I feel. This is nothing like the last place I called home in Manhattan. Back then Alexa was my roommate before she moved in with Noah. Once she left, I found another girl to share the expenses with right away. After I'd bolted back to Boston, my room was quickly handed over to the next person with a rent check in hand.

She picks up a dated rug that is thrown on the hardwood floors. "I like that it's furnished."

I do too. It's not my ideal neighborhood. The décor looks like it came right out of the eighties, but it's comfortable and safe. "I think I should take it."

"Do you need me to help you with the damage deposit or first month's rent?"

It's a question born out of our friendship, not her desire to get me out of her place. "I can handle it."

"You're sure?" she asks through a smile. "I want to help if I can."

I reach for her shoulders, pulling her into a warm embrace. "You've helped me a lot the past two weeks."

"You've lost weight." Her eyes rake over my thin frame. "You're skinnier now than you were when you got here."

I am. I haven't had an appetite. Food, sleep and a quiet mind have been in short supply. Even though Alexa has cooked delicious meals for me the past few weeks I haven't been able to stomach the taste. I'm not sick. Physically, there's nothing wrong with me. I finally feel as though I'm being lifted out of the fog of emotions that I experienced after my break up with Parker. I can see the future now, even if it means moving into this apartment that is three subway stops away from her place.

"We'll go out to celebrate your new place with Noah tonight." She claps her hands together. "I can fix you up with someone from work if you want to make it a double date."

I visibly wince at the words. "I'm not into teachers," I tease.

"This one is hot. His name is Doug. You'll like him."

I study her face. There's a hopeful glint in her eyes. She wants this for me. She wants to push me into my future with full force. "What does he look like?" It's shallow but it's important. The last thing I want is to be with a man who physically resembles Parker in any way.

The question doesn't rattle her at all. "He's about average height I guess. He's got blonde hair, and blue eyes." Her hand darts to her chin. "He has a beard and he's ripped."

"How would you know if he's ripped?" I tap my foot against the faded throw rug. "You're making that up."

She pats me on my elbow. "I'm not." She grins. "He wears tight t-shirts sometimes. All I can say is wow."

"Wow?" I parrot back.

"Wow," she repeats, her brows jumping up.

"I don't know, Lex." The knot that is overtaking my stomach is reason enough for me to derail this plan. "It's really soon."

"It's a dinner." She pushes my hair back over my shoulders. "One dinner. It's not like you're marrying the guy."

"I'll do it," I whisper. "I guess I'll do it."

Chapter 5

Doug gestures towards Noah with a nod of his chin. "What's with his face?"

Any desire that may have been edging its way to the surface is lost with that one question. "What do you mean?" I whisper back. "What are you talking about?"

I know exactly what he means. Noah Foster was stabbed years ago and now the ever-present reminder of that juts down the length of his face. I've grown so accustomed to it that I don't even register it anymore when I look at him. It doesn't define him in any way but brash, thoughtless comments like the ones that Doug just made tear through Noah still. I've seen it happen in the past.

"Something is wrong with his face."

Something is wrong with your sense of decency, jerk.

"It's a scar," I point out the obvious.

"How did he get that?"

Alexa turns her attention away from Noah to lock eyes with me. She's sitting next to Doug. There's absolutely no way she hasn't tuned in to the current conversation Doug is straining to have with me.

"Do you like being a teacher?" I pull the question out of the back of my mind because I don't want to make a scene. Axel NY is one of the most expensive restaurants in Manhattan. It's a place where you wear your Sunday best and put on a brilliant smile.

"It's alright." He reaches for his water glass. His arm brushes against mine and I feel absolutely nothing from the touch.

"Doug received the teacher of the month award in January," Alexa chimes in. "It's kind of a big deal."

"Congratulations," I offer because it's expected. This is a mistake. I wish I were back in my bed at Alexa's apartment. I knew it was too soon to venture into the dating world again. I was happy just sitting back watching that world pass me by.

"Sure, thanks." His eyes scan the room before they settle on me.

"Kayla just got a new job." Alexa is bound and determined to push this date over a cliff. Is it not obvious by the way I'm avoiding eye contact with him that I'm not having the time of my life here?

"Do you have a sister?" His fingers glide over mine.

I pull my hand back so abruptly that my wine glass teeters precariously for a second before I reach to balance it. "Why?"

Noah clears his throat looking for someone's attention. I'll happily give him mine. I look up and our eyes lock. He cocks a brow before a wide grin overtakes his handsome face. "Kayla has a brother."

I'm surprised that he knows that much about me. Our conversations have always involved Alexa. "Damn." Doug's fist hits the table lightly. "I have a friend who is looking for a girl just like you. I thought if you had a sister we could all hang out."

If I had a sister I'd hide her in a closet until the perfect man came into her life. Dating sucks.

"Sorry." I shrug scanning the room in hopes I'll find the waiter so I can order something strong enough to get me through the dessert course.

"I have a sister," Alexa offers because she's always the extra helpful one. "She's married though."

"What about you, Noah?" Doug's eyes blaze a path across Noah's face. "Do you have a sister?"

"I don't." He taps his finger on the edge of the table. "I have a brother."

"He has a twin brother." Alexa turns sharply to stare at him. "A fraternal twin brother I've never met."

He tilts his head towards her before scooping her hand in his. "We're not close."

"I'm still waiting for you to explain that to me." Her voice cracks.

"We'll talk about it later." Noah's deep voice carries softly over the table. "Now is not the time."

Her head bows towards her lap. I watch her shoulders quiver. I want to reach to comfort her but Doug is in the way. She's told me about Noah's brother. I've heard the story about how he offered the information with a caveat about how they haven't spoken to one another in years. He's not a part of Noah's life. Alexa's love for Noah runs deep. She wants to understand every facet of who he is, including the brother that he'd rather forget.

"Alexa?" I whisper her name in her direction.

"I'm fine." The words don't match her body language at all. She's gripping the linen napkin that was beside her plate in her hands, wringing it recklessly. "Will he come to our wedding? It's only three months away now. You should fix things with him before then."

Noah shakes his head slightly as a muted curse word leaves his lips. "I'm not having this conversation here, Alexa."

"I'm not having it unless it's here. We have to send out the invitations soon." Her head juts up. Her expression is stoic and determined. I've seen that look before. Alexa is out for answers and Noah is going to have to give them to her.

"Maybe we should go." I reach to grab Doug's hand and instantly regret it. It suggests I want to be alone with him. I don't want that. As much as I want to chase away Parker's memory, Doug isn't going to help me do that. I'm not attracted to him at all.

He's on his feet in an instant. "We can go to my place."

Um, no. No, we cannot.

"Stay." Noah's hand flies over the table. "Don't take off."

I look to Alexa for confirmation of his words. She's frustrated. I can see it when her eyes meet mine.

"I think we should go," I whisper as I follow Doug's lead and pull myself to my feet, teetering slightly in the nude heels I paired with the navy dress I have on.

I stare at Alexa seeing gratitude there. She's taken so much pride in the openness within her relationship with Noah. The knowledge that he has a brother that she's never met pains her because soon his twin will be her family too.

"We'll see you at home later?" Noah nods towards me, the words filled with a trace of warmth.

I look at Doug and his overly eager grin. Fuck. I have to walk out of this restaurant with him and keep myself occupied for a few hours before I can go back to Alexa and Noah's place. They need time alone. It's only another two days until I move into my own apartment but right now that feels like an endless eternity. "I'll be there."

"This way, my lady." Doug pulls my arm through his. "I'm going to give you an evening you'll never forget."

Great. This evening has officially gone from bad to hell.

Chapter 6

"I thought we'd go back to my place."

His hand snakes around my waist as the words leave his lips. We've been in this club for more than an hour and my plan to distract Doug with the numerous women all bumping and grinding against him hasn't worked at all. He's still hell bent on taking me back to his apartment.

"This is so fun," I lie through clenched teeth. This is not fun at all. I have to be at work at eight in the morning. I'm tired. I'm aggravated and I'm sick of feeling Doug's hands pawing all over my semi expensive dress.

His breath feels hot over my neck. "We'd have more fun if were alone. I'd love to screw you."

You'd love to screw me? Aren't you a gentleman? Images of a quick few thrusts before he passes out on top of me flash across my mind.

"You should dance." I point towards a group of women gathered on the dance floor. They came to get fucked, or in Doug's case screwed by a teacher. "Get out there."

"Nah." His hand moves higher racing over the bottom of my breast. "Let's go."

"I'm not going home with you." I take a step forward. "It's not happening."

He's around me in an instant, his hands latching tightly to my hips. "I'm not asking for anything but a roll in the hay."

An actual, literal roll in the hay would likely feel better than climbing all over his hot, sweaty body at this point. "You're a nice guy but I'm not interested."

"Why not?" he snaps. "What's wrong with me?"

It's a question that deserves an honest answer. I don't have one. It's not that he's not attractive. Many women would chase after him in a heartbeat. It's not that sex with him wouldn't be fun. It might actually be better than I'm envisioning. It's just that there's nothing there. I feel absolutely no draw towards him. Jumping into bed for the sake of feeling wanted isn't something I can do anymore.

"There's nothing wrong with you," I say assuredly. "You're great. I'm just not ready yet."

"Is it because of a break up?" His bottom lip juts out in a frown. "Did you dump your boyfriend?"

I glance into his eyes and see a flash of understanding. "Something like that," I offer back. It's semantics at this point. It doesn't matter whether Parker dumped me or I dumped him. What matters is that it's over.

"That's killer." His hand darts to his chest. "My girlfriend dumped me for another guy last year. I'm still getting over it."

Who knew? Who knew that we shared a similar pain?

"Does it get easier?" I lean in closer. "Does the pain go away?"

He nods as his hand races to my arm. "Every day it gets better."

I want to believe him. I do believe him. I feel better today than I felt when I first stepped off the plane weeks ago.

"So?" The words hold way too much expectation. "My place?"

I brush my lips softly across his cheek before taking a step back. "Not a chance."

***

I exit the club onto the street and into the late, cool evening air. I shiver slightly wishing I had thought far enough ahead to grab a sweater before I left Alexa's apartment hours ago. My eyes scan the scene outside the club. It's near midnight now and the throngs of people waiting in line to get inside have only increased. The hum of their voices as they mingle and connect before ever hitting the dance floor wafts through the air. I don't know how I'm going to jump back into that. I'll need to at some point. Meeting men in Manhattan isn't as easy as it looks.

"Kayla?"

The voice that calls my name is rough and deep. It's not Doug. This voice carries more confidence. I whip around on my heel, my eyes scanning over the crowd behind me. I don't recognize any of the faces.

"Kayla." It calls to me again, louder this time. A hand juts above a group of people standing near the entrance to the club.

I step towards the voice trying desperately to place it. I briefly dated a few men before I moved back to Boston. Right now, I can't recall any of them. Please let it be someone from work.

He steps forward, the crowd parting to let him through. I notice her first. She's a beautiful brunette, slightly taller than I am, her hand clenched tightly in his. She's wearing a fitted red dress, the neckline so low that her cleavage is on display. Her lipstick is bold. It matches the hue of the dress. She flashes a set of perfect white teeth before her gaze travels up to his face.

"Ben," I say his name for the first time.

He leans forward to brush his lips over my cheek. "It's great to see you."

I step back out of sheer need. My body aches just from the soft touch of his lips on my skin. "It's nice to see you too."

"Who is this?" The woman attached to his hand nods towards me, her voice shaded with a European accent. "How do you know her?"

"This is Kayla." His hand drops hers. "We met a few weeks ago."

She stares at him. "Where did you meet?"

His eyes don't leave my face. "It was on a flight from Boston."

I instantly see relief wash over her. "You're visiting New York?" Her hand reaches to skim over my arm. "You like it here?"

"I live here now." I don't move even though her touch is making me incredibly uncomfortable. Her reaction to his vague response about us meeting on a flight quieted something within her. She was jealous. I could sense it within her eyes but it's gone now.

"Really?" She claps her hands together as if that's the best news she's heard all day. "Do you need a guide to show you around?"

Great. The girlfriend of the best fuck I've ever had wants to be my bestie. I shouldn't have gotten out of bed today.

"Kayla has lived here before." His tone is low.

I turn my head to look at him. He's exactly as I remember him save for the stubble that's now covering his jaw. He's dressed differently though. Gone are the designer suits. Tonight he's dressed in a black sweater and jeans. I'm not sure I would have recognized him if I spotted him in the crowd.

"I'm Mickey." Her hand darts into mine. "It's nice to meet you."

"Kayla," I say my name even though I know she's well aware of it. "It's good to meet you too."

"You'll come inside for a drink, yes?" She motions towards the entrance of the club.

I glance at it briefly before I shake my head. "No. I'm actually on my way home. I was already inside."

"That's a shame." Her overzealous pout isn't lost on me. There's another wave of relief washing over her. She wants Ben to herself. I can't blame her.

"Have fun," I say without any meaning at all attached to it. She's going to go into that club and dance with him, then she'll get into a bed with him and experience all the pleasure I felt. Damn her. Damn my life right now.

"Another time, yes?" She leans forward before her lips brush against my left cheek, and then the right.

"Sure thing." I look towards the street in search of an available taxi. "I need to be going."

Ben's hand reaches for my elbow just as I turn to leave. "Let me hail you a cab, Kayla."

"That's not necessary," I quip. I don't want to prolong my internal agony for another moment. It's torturous knowing my moment with him has passed. I don't want to remember the way his body felt as he took me in that bed. I can't think about the way his lips tasted as they pulled my desire to the surface.

"I insist." His breath roams across my shoulder. "I'll find you inside, Mickey."

With an animated sigh she turns to rejoin the group. Her silence is a clear indicator that he'll need to do damage control once he's said goodnight to me.

"You don't need to do this," I say as I walk towards the crowded curb.

He leans into me, his hand circling my waist. "We'll have more luck if we walk a block over."

I study his face, taking in the smooth lines. His dark eyes are warm. His mouth is curved into an easy smile.

"Are you settling into life in New York?" He pushes his hands into the front pockets of his dark jeans as he slows to walk at my pace.

I nod. "I am." I don't see the benefit in adding more details. He's being a gentleman. I knew it was part of the fabric of who he was the moment he held the door of the car open for me at the airport.

"You found a place to stay?" It's a question that isn't grounded in curiosity about my current address. The way his eyes are darting over the faces of the people we pass speaks of how little he's invested in my answer.

I motion towards a cab barrelling down Lexington Avenue. "I'll grab that one."

His hand is on my elbow before I can take a step towards the street. "Not yet."

"Not yet?" My heart quickens in my chest. "Why?"

He stops mid step, leaning in close to me. I feel his lips brush over mine in a lush, intimate kiss. The moan the escapes him flows into my body.

On that crowded street in the center of the city, with people rushing around us, I pull my hand into his hair, and kiss him back. It's everything I remember from my first night back in the city. My sex clenches when his tongue pushes between my lips. My body aches when his hand floats along my back to the curve above my ass and my heart stops when I feel his hard cock press into my stomach.

"Come back to the hotel with me." The words fall from him in a heated rush as his lips trail over my neck. "I need to taste you."

I exhale sharply, my breath flowing out in jagged spurts. "I can't." I shake my head.

"You can." His mouth is on my skin again, grazing along my cheek. "I want to be inside of you."

"Mickey," I say her name. "You have a girlfriend."

I feel his hand clench into a fist on my back. "No. She's not that."

I push against him to no avail. My hands rest on his chest. "She's your girlfriend."

"No," he repeats the protest. "Mickey is just a woman I sometimes…"

I don't want to hear the word. I don't want the image floating into my thoughts the next time I'm in the bed touching myself while I think about him. "I need to go home."

"Let's go for a drink." He pushes his hands into my hair. "Please don't go. I've thought about you for weeks. Tonight is the first night I've been out since then. It's fate that we're here together."

I want the words to have truth woven into them. I stare at him. He knows what he's doing to me. He knows that his hands bring up needs that only he can satisfy. He sees the untethered desire that I feel for him floating over my expression. It's there. It's not hidden or veiled beneath anything.

"Kayla," he says my name into my lips. "I can't let you go yet."

I lean forward knowing that I should get in the next taxi that passes by us. I push my lips into his fearing that after tonight I'll never see him again. I cup his cheek in my hand as I give in to the desire and the desperate need that is inside of me to taste him one last time.

"What the hell are you doing, Ben?" I hear her voice behind me. It's shrill, it's loud and it penetrates the one moment in time I want to last.

"Shit," he says through a nervous chuckle. "Let's get out of here."

He reaches for my hand, pulling it into his. I fumble with my clutch trying to keep up with him as we both laugh out loud at Mickey's curse filled rant wafting through the air behind us. I turn to look back. I feel my heel catch in a sidewalk grate. My hand escapes his, as my purse flies into the air and my face hits the pavement with a dull and empty thud.

Chapter 7

"Kayla. Kayla, can you hear me?" A woman's voice tears through the immeasurable pain in my head. It sounds as though she's screaming at me. What the hell is her problem?

My eyes dart open and I'm instantly aware that I'm not in bed at Alexa's. This room is bright. The large light above my head is shining directly into my face.

"Kayla. Kayla Monroe?" She repeats my name. "Do you know your name?"

If I didn't, I'd guess it was Kayla Monroe just by her incessant need to repeat it over and over again to me.

"Yes," I whisper through a swollen lip. "I'm Kayla."

Her hand brushes over my forehead. "Don't move. I'll get the doctor."

"The doctor?" I try to raise my hand to touch my forehead. It's burning. I feel as though I fell asleep with my face inside of a frying pan. "What doctor?"

I sense movement beside me. Where's Alexa? I need her.

"Kayla?" It's a man now. His voice is deep and gentle. It's familiar.

I turn my head slowly towards him. I remember him. He's handsome. We kissed. "Ben," I say his name. I remember his name.

"You're going to be fine." He leans down to run his finger over my lip. "Nothing is broken. You didn't need any stitches."

"Why are you here?" I try to look behind him for another familiar face. "Did I get hurt?"

He nods slowly, his eyes darting beside me to a nurse standing next to the bed. I don't flinch as she grips my wrist to take my pulse.

"Her pulse is ninety-two." I listen as she shuffles with papers. "She's stabilizing."

"Give her four hundred milligrams of ibuprofen and get someone from admitting down here," Ben directs her. "She needs to be monitored tonight."

Why is he saying those things? I turn to watch her walk quickly past one of the curtains that surrounds the bed. I'm in the hospital. I try to sit up. I can't be here. I need to be at work in the morning. I need to tell Alexa where I am so she doesn't panic.

"I have to go." I try to swing my legs over the side of the bed. "I need to go home."

"You can't leave." His hands push me back down. "You're seriously hurt."

"I want to talk to the doctor." I feel my lip quiver. "Go get the doctor."

He shakes his head slightly. I watch him take a heavy swallow. "I'm your doctor."

"What?" I bolt back to a sitting position.

He steadies my balance with his hands on my shoulders. "You fell, Kayla. I brought you here. I'm your attending physician."

"You're not a doctor," I blurt the words out quickly without any thought. I don't know who he is. Could he be a doctor?

"I'm a doctor." He points to the identification badge clipped to the front of his sweater. "I work here."

My eyes scan the badge. I can't focus on the writing. It's blurry. "This isn't real." I feel panic race through me.

"I'm Dr. Ben Foster."

"Foster?" I shake my head certain that I misheard him. "As in the Noah Foster?"

"No, Ben Foster. I'm not Noah. Noah is a photographer. You probably saw a story about him online or in one of the papers," he says gruffly. "My name is Ben. You and I met several weeks ago. You may feel temporarily confused because of the impact of your fall. That will…"

"Do you know Noah Foster?" I interrupt him.

"Do you know him?" It's a challenge woven into a nervous chuckle.

My eyes don't leave his face. He knows Noah. I see it now. That's who he looks like. "I know him," I offer quietly. "He loves my best friend."

"Noah is in love?"

I nod slowly. "You're related to Noah, aren't you? You look like him."

His expression doesn't change but his eyes give something away. "You need to rest."

My hand darts to my mouth and I wince at the brush of my fingers against my swollen lip. "You're him, aren't you?"

I see the resignation in his expression the moment the question leaves my lips. "I'm who?" he asks, frustration lacing his tone. "Who do you think I am?"

"You're Noah's twin brother."

He scrubs the back of his neck with his right hand. "Yes. Noah Foster is my brother."

"I live with him," I offer although the moment I say the words I realize the implied meaning in them.

"You what?" His brow cocks with the question. "You live with my brother?"

I pull my hands together as I see the nurse push the curtain aside again. This time she's holding a rectangular tray in her hands. She reaches to hand me a paper cup containing two small pills. I tenderly take it, popping both of them into my mouth. She replaces the cup with one filled with water. I grimace as the liquid touches my open lip before I swallow it. The bitter taste of blood floats over my tongue.

"I need you to call Noah," I say as much to the nurse as to Ben. "He'll be worried about where I am. I mean, Alexa will be worried."

Ben's hand flies over me towards the nurse. "I'll handle this."

She hesitates before she turns on her heel, walks towards the curtain and disappears behind it. I lean back instantly aware that I have to explain to Alexa that I had a one night stand with Noah's brother. He's the brother that she's been longing to meet for months and I hooked up with him.

"I can't believe you're Noah's brother," I mutter the words. "They were just talking about you tonight."

"Who was talking about me?" He doesn't raise his eyes to meet mine. He's holding a tablet in his hands, his fingers jutting over the screen quickly.

"Noah and his fiancé." My eyes sting with tears. My head is throbbing, my lip feels bigger than my entire face and I know that tomorrow my new job will be in jeopardy because Vivian won't have anyone to run to the corner deli to get her a sandwich. "Can I please just go home?"

"Wait." His index finger taps my hand. "Did you just say Noah is engaged?"

Why am I the one providing all of this information to him? Shouldn't Noah be sharing the news of his impending marriage with his twin brother? I don't want to be caught in the middle of this. It's bad enough that I have to explain to Alexa and Noah that I crawled into bed with Ben without knowing his last name. I'm ashamed, I'm embarrassed and I want to get this entire mess out in the open as soon as I can.

"When is he getting married?" His fingers brush against my forehead. "What's she like?"

I can't do this. I feel as though I'm betraying Lex. I'm giving this man information that should be coming from her. "You should talk to Noah."

His hand leaps to his own forehead. His index finger traces a pointed path along his brow. "I haven't spoken to Noah in years. I can't talk to him."

My loyalty isn't to him. Once I walk through the doors of this hospital and back into my life, our connection will cease to exist. I'm a one night stand with a complication in the form of a head wound. "I can't talk about Noah to you. I need to call him and Alexa now."

"Is there someone else you can call?" he asks, pulling on the collar of his sweater.

"No," I concede. "I'm staying with them. They'll be worried about me."

He exhales audibly. "Let me think for a minute."

I sense immediately the anxiety that has overtaken him. It's the same reaction Noah had at the restaurant when Alexa pressed him about his brother.

"Just please let me call them." I sit up swiftly again, my hand bolting to the edge of the bed for stability. "Can't they take care of me tonight?"

The darkness around his eyes lifts. "No, but I can."

Chapter 8

"I thought you were going to take me to the hotel." I hold steady to his arm as he guides me into an apartment with a Park Avenue address. "You live here, don't you?"

"Yes," he quietly acquiesces. "That hotel is a shit hole. I won't stay there."

The words bite although they shouldn't. This is the place he raced to after he'd fucked me that night weeks ago. He'd left me there because I was a random that wasn't worthy of this.

I stay silent as he flips on the light switch. The room fills with warm light giving me my first glimpse into his real world. The space is opulent and masculine. Rich dark furniture sets the tone. Beautiful artwork hangs from the walls, which are painted a deep shade of gray. It matches what I imagined it to be to a tee.

"What did Noah say when you called him?" His hand is pressing on my lower back, guiding me further into the space.

I'm surprised by his restraint. He'd stood just feet away from me near the entrance to the hospital as I called Alexa. She hadn't answered so I left a brief voicemail telling her that I was out for the night but would be home after work tomorrow. Ben's insistence that he call my boss, Vivian, in the morning directly to explain what happened quashed my fears about my job. He'd explain my injuries and my need for rest. I'd be back at the office the day after tomorrow, no worse for wear.

"I didn't speak to him." I run my hand across my forehead. "How long do I have to wear this bandage?"

"Did you talk... did you talk to his fiancé?" He clears his throat. "Alexa, right?"

I nod slowly. Watching his mouth move as her names leaves his lips seems foreign to me. "I left her a message."

"You need to rest." His hand circles my waist. "I can help you undress and get into bed."

I feel exposed at the mention of getting undressed. "I can do it myself."

"No." His hand motions towards a hallway. "I'll help."

I don't argue the point. It's not as though he hasn't seen me nude before. Besides that, he's a doctor. Christ, he's a fucking doctor and Noah's brother. I still can't fathom how I went from sitting next to a stranger on a flight to standing in the apartment of Noah's twin waiting for him to undress me.

"How long have you known him?" His hand brushes over the zipper at the back of my dress as we enter a dimly lit bedroom.

"Noah?"

He pushes his hands over my shoulders, grabbing the neckline of the dress. "When did you meet him?"

"A year ago," I sigh as his hands skim my skin taking the dress with them. "Maybe it was longer."

His breath catches as my white bra and panties come into full view. "Is he happy?"

I close my eyes when I feel his fingers deftly undo the clasp of my bra. "Yes, he's happy."

His hands move down, gliding over my stomach before stopping at the edge of my panties. "What's she like?"

I lean back into him. My body betraying my need to stay focused in the moment. "Alexa?"

"Yes." He takes a step forward, pulling me into him. "Is she like you?"

I chuckle at the thought. "We're not the same."

He turns me around effortlessly until I'm facing him. "Is she good to him?"

"She loves him," I offer. "You should meet her. You'd like her."

He shakes his head. "I can't," he murmurs.

"Why?" I reach for his arm, a wave of dizziness overtaking me. "I need to sit."

"No." His lips graze across my forehead. "You need to sleep."

I don't protest as he helps me into a king size bed. I snuggle into the sheets, reveling in the softness of their touch against my bare skin. "I'm tired," I whimper into the pillow.

"I'll need to wake you during the night." His breath traces across my neck. "I'll be gentle."

I barely hear the words as my mind quiets and the gentle hum of sleep overtakes me.

***

"Do you remember anything from last night?" His lips are almost touching mine.

I lazily open my eyes to see his face. His head is resting gently on the pillow next to me. His hair pushed into a matted mess. How can he look this gorgeous after sleeping?   "Your girlfriend was chasing us." I push my bottom lip out. "Her name is Minnie or Donald, something like that."

He pushes his tongue into his top lip to hold back a grin. "She's not my girlfriend and her name is Mickey."

"Right." I dip my chin in his direction. "She's your girlfriend."

"I've fucked her once or twice months ago."

"You can't remember how many times?" I pull the sheet around me.

"Honestly, no, I can't remember how many times or even what it was like." He shrugs. "We were just going to have some fun at the club with a few of her friends."

"She's territorial." It's a polite way of saying she's certifiably nuts.

"She's bat shit crazy." A wide grin takes over his mouth. "I deleted her number from my phone. I need to stay as far away from her as I can."

I reach up to run my hand over my forehead. "When can I take the bandage off?"

"I'll check on it shortly." He moves closer, the smooth skin of his chest resting against my breasts. "Tell me how you're feeling."

"My head hurts." I close my eyes, finding instant relief from the pain. "Will the headaches last long?"

"I'll get you something for that." He pulls back, swinging his long legs over the edge of the bed.

I watch in silence as he stands. His nude body is on display. He doesn't try to shield anything as he leaves the room. I close my eyes until I hear his footsteps near the doorway again.

I don't argue as he helps me sit up. I take the two pills he hands me without question, washing them down with a long swallow from a chilled bottle of water.

"That will help." He pushes gently on my shoulders. "Rest your head."

I give in to the desire to sink back into the comfort of his bed. "Do you walk around in the nude often?"

"That's a strange question." He tips the bottle of water in my direction before taking a hearty mouthful. "Do you?"

"Noah does," I offer.

"You've seen Noah naked?" He cocks a brow.

"No." I shake my head before I realize the movement isn't helping matters. I feel as though my brain is jumbled. The pain is constant, throbbing and clouding my clear thoughts. "Alexa used to talk about it when they first got together."

He rounds the bed, sliding his tall frame back under the covers. "He wore clothes when I knew him." The meaning behind the words isn't lost on me. He doesn't feel that he knows Noah anymore. I feel a sense of sadness for both of them.

"When's the last time you saw him?" I don't expect an answer to the question. I don't even know why I asked it.

"I can't remember." He glides his body closer to mine. "It's been many years."

"Do you miss him?" I ask, trying desperately to keep my eyes open.

His lips brush over the tip of my nose. "Sleep, Kayla."

I nod. I can't refuse the request. My body won't let me.

Chapter 9

"I've thought about the way you taste since I met you that night."

I keep my eyes closed. I know that I should be telling him that I can't do this. I know that since I've learned that he's Noah's brother that virtually everything I thought about him has changed, but in this one solitary instant in time, I don't want to carry any knowledge of his connection to Noah. I want to forget it. I want to just be Kayla and I want him to just be Ben.

"Open your eyes, Kayla." His lips feather soft over my cheek. "Let me see your beautiful blue eyes."

I lift my eyelids to peer directly into his intense brown eyes. "What time is it?"

"It's after noon." His hand moves over my breast to my stomach. "You've been asleep for hours."

"My boss." I'm not panicked. He promised he'd call her after I gave him the number last night.

"Vivian." His tongue darts out to trace a path over my bottom lip. "I spoke to her. I explained what happened. You have tomorrow off too."

I'm grateful. I shouldn't be. It's essentially his fault that I smashed my head into the sidewalk. His jealous lover decided to confront us on that street when I lost my footing. "I need to go home now."

"Soon." His hand inches lower, skirting over the top of my panties. "I'll take you there soon."

I nod and close my eyes briefly, letting a slow puff of air escape my lips. "We need to talk about…"

The words are lost within his kiss. His lips are aggressive and smooth as they claim mine. His tongue pushes into my mouth, parting my lips slightly to give it better access. He's as skilled at kissing as he is at fucking.

His hand pushes my panties down slowly, inching them down my long, slim legs. "You're wet for me. You've been wet since I kissed you on the street last night."

The image of that moment floats back into my mind. He promised me one last night in his bed. I wanted it then. So much has changed since then but not my desire for him.

He shifts his body suddenly until he's hovering above me. I look up into his face. I see only small glimpses of Noah there now. I see more of Ben. They're not identical. His jaw is softer than Noah's, his nose broader. Their eyes are the same though. I see the same tortured past in Ben's gaze that I see when I study Noah.

He lowers his head to my breast, pulling my nipple between his teeth. I moan automatically from the touch. His mouth jumps to my stomach as he pulls back his tall frame.

"You're ready for me." His lips touch my smooth folds. "Your cunt is so perfect. It's so wet."

I don't resist as he pulls my legs over his shoulders, his face diving into me. I lean back, my hands gripping the sheets on the bed as his tongue hones in on my clit, circling it with just the right amount of pressure. I close my eyes, riding the unending wave of pleasure that he's giving to me. His tongue pulls me close to the edge, before I settle back down, nearing the brink but not crossing over.

"I want to come," I whimper the words. "I need to."

"You will." He pulls back slightly, pushing a mouthful of air onto my aching clitoris. "You're so swollen, Kayla. You're so close."

My hips buck off the bed, my body in search of his mouth. "Lick it, Ben," I say his name in a heated rush. "Lick it."

"I'll make you come all over my face." He laps at me hungrily, pulling me closer to the orgasm I so desperately need.

"Like that," I call out. "God, yes, like that."

He doesn't stop when I push him away as the pleasure washes through me. He doesn't give in to my insistent pleas to stop after I crash back down. He licks, tempts and pulls another climax from within me before he finally stops, resting his head against my breasts.

"I wish I could fuck you right now." His breath flows across my chilled skin. "I want so badly to feel your cunt around me."

I want that too. I stroke my hand through his hair. "Fuck me," I murmur into the quiet room. "I want it."

He crawls up my body, his long, hard cock rubbing along my

leg as he pulls himself up. "I don't have any condoms in my apartment. I don't fuck women here."

Any disappointment I may have felt at the loss of the promise of his cock inside of me is replaced by the quiet satisfaction in knowing that women don't find comfort here. They don't wrap themselves around him while he sleeps. He keeps this part of his life separate and removed from what he does in that small, cramped hotel room.

I don't care that I landed here because I was hurt and the intuitive parts of him that were born to heal want to care for me. I don't care that he sacrificed his sanctuary to keep Noah from finding out about us. I don't care that everything about his life has overlapped and pierced mine.

My hand drops to his thigh, fishing forward searching for his cock. "I can suck you off." The words sound dirty and needy. My breath is still staggered from the high he took me to.

"I have to go to work soon." His lips push into mine stealing a moist, slow kiss. "I want to hold you for a minute."

I move slightly when he lowers himself onto the bed next to me. He scoops his strong arms around me pulling me into his chest. I breathe in the fragrance of his skin, a potent combination of cologne, sweat and my scent.

"I hate that you know him," he whispers into my hair. "I hate that you're part of his life."

Chapter 10

I walk back into the bedroom after soaking my weary body in the strong spray of his shower for the past fifteen minutes. He's dressed in grey slacks and a blue dress shirt. His hair is pushed back from his forehead. He looks different. The authoritative parts of him are on full display in his expression.

"I bought you some clothes when you were asleep earlier." He waves towards a plain white bag sitting atop the bed. "I can't send you home wearing that dress."

I smile at the thoughtful promise that is hidden beneath the gesture. I open the bag, carefully pulling each garment from within it. Dark wash jeans, a white blouse, new black panties and a pair of flats, size eight.

"How did you know my sizes?" That should have been an immediate thank you but the fact that each piece of clothing is perfectly sized strikes me. It speaks of a familiar and comfortable knowledge that we haven't shared.

He takes a heavy step closer. My instinct should be to back away. He's tall, muscular, imposing in a way that screams of the care he takes in bed and his desperate need to bring a woman the pleasure that he knows lives within her. I don't flinch as he pulls the towel I've wrapped around me to the ground.

"I've memorized the shape of your hips." He picks up the panties and kneels swiftly, motioning for me to hold onto his shoulder as he lifts my legs, one at a time, carefully pulling the smooth, silk fabric up my legs. He follows their trail with his hands, adjusting them over the curve of my ass before his face brushes softly against my crotch.

He's on his feet now reaching for the jeans. "When I fucked you that first night, you wrapped your beautiful legs around me."

"I remember," I offer quietly.

He helps me step into the jeans, gliding them effortlessly up my legs. "I remember the pressure of your knees on my sides as you clenched yourself around me. Your body fits so perfectly with mine."

He reaches down to clasp them shut, pulling the zipper into place.

"Your tits are just the right size." The bra I was wearing under my dress is in his hands now. He pulls it over my breasts, adjusting the flesh within the fabric before he reaches behind me, hooking it closed.

I watch as he picks up the blouse and wraps it around my body. "When I was walking down the aisle towards my seat on the plane that night, I saw your face."

My eyes bolt up to meet his. "I don't remember seeing you before you sat down."

"You were looking to the side. There was a man sitting across the aisle from you." His hands rest on my shoulders briefly before he begins buttoning the blouse. "I saw the way you were looking at him. I saw the way he was looking at you."

I push back to that place in time. I don't recall any face but Ben's. The moment he sat next to me, the electrical currents in my brain piled into overdrive. He had turned to look at me and I knew in that moment that he was unlike any man I'd ever been near. The raw confidence that seeped through his voice had captivated me instantly. If I hadn't gone to that hotel room with him I would have spent half the night in the bed in Alexa's guest room with my hand pressed between my legs imagining the taste and feel of his body.

"I can't remember," I offer as his fingers fly over the buttons fastening them. "I don't remember any man but you."

"Good." His voice carries relief that's not overt. "I wanted you the moment I saw you. I had to fuck you that night."

I had to fuck him too. I wanted to fuck him still. Any question of this being a random one night stand has been erased in the past twenty four hours. This man is now part of my life.

***

"I'm doing rounds and I'm already running late." His eyes scan the expensive watch on his wrist. "I've arranged for a car to take you to Noah's."

Shit. Noah. I'll see Noah soon.

"Thank you," I say because it's necessary. It fills the space where I should be telling him that I'm going to talk to Noah about him. I have to.

"Kayla." His hand brushes across my cheek. The pain that was there immediately after my fall is dull now. It's become a quiet ache in the background. My reflection in the bathroom mirror was comforting. I don't look nearly as bad as my imagination lead me to believe I would. It's obvious something happened but I can explain it to Alexa. She'll understand.

"I need to tell him that I know you." Mincing words at this point seems trite and unnecessary. We both know that I'm obligated to Noah.

His head shakes slightly. "I don't want you to tell him about me."

I don't want to have the conversation either but I owe Noah. I can't walk back into his home and not reveal the fact that I've been sharing a bed with his twin brother. That's not who I am. I can't do that to Noah, but more than that, I can't do that to Alexa. She has been the one person in my life who has been steady and composed the last few weeks. "I have to tell him."

"I want to tell him." He pushes his hands into the pockets of his pants. "Let me tell him, please."

There's no need to offer a plea. "You'll talk to him?"

"Yes." There's nothing more to sustain his answer. He doesn't elaborate.

"When?" I push because I need to. I'll be leaving Alexa and Noah's home tomorrow to settle into the small, one bedroom in Murray Hill. My life will no longer be connected so literally to theirs, but I'm part of their family and they are part of mine. A secret this size can't be tucked away in a corner. It builds in size every day. It increases in depth when it's willfully ignored. I don't want what I have with Ben to end. There's a whisper of promise there that I want to nurture.

"Come back and talk to me tomorrow." He takes a step towards the door. "I really need to get to work."

My stomach tangles in a knot so big I fear I'll trip over it if I move. "You want me to go back there and not say anything?"

"I want you to trust that I'll tell him soon." It's a morsel meant to placate me.

I stare into his face. His expression is unreadable. He's asking me to entrust my friendship with Alexa into his hands. They are hands that I barely know but want desperately to believe in. "I don't know."

"Kayla." His hands jump to my face, cupping my cheeks within them. "I need a bit of time to process this. I promise I'll talk to him soon."

I want to see the truth behind the words when I look into his eyes. I need to. I bow my head in acceptance fearing that the silent promise I just made will cost me Alexa's love and friendship if she ever finds out that I already know Noah's twin brother. All of this may ruin our connection forever.

Chapter 11

"Doug said you didn't go home with him." Her voice is behind me. I hadn't closed the door to my bedroom when I raced into the apartment and down the hall. I knew I was alone the moment my key unhinged the lock. The space was quiet and empty.

I turn around to greet her. "He just wanted to have sex with me."

"Don't all men just want to have sex?" She blinks through a smile. "Is your face bruised?"

I instinctively want to retreat as she walks towards me. "I tripped and fell."

"What?" Her hand dashes over my cheek, skimming the edge of a bruise. "When did you fall?"

"When I thought I could wear heels on a sidewalk grate." I pull her hand into mine. If she pushes my hair away from my forehead, she'll see the abrasion. I don't want that.

Her face lights up with a smile. "I've done that too. I fell into a hotdog vendor's cart a few months ago."

I laugh at the vision of that. "You're lucky he didn't sue you."

"I know, right?" She pats my forearm. "You're home early. Did you go to work today?"

Lying to Alexa isn't a path I want to venture down. I'm sure she's told me her fair share of small white lies, just as I have to her since we met. If I make a decision to lie now, I'll be changing the entire course of our friendship. "I can pick up my keys to my apartment in an hour."

She raises her eyebrows at me. "Seriously? I'll come with you."

"I'm excited to have my own place." I continue the detour around the subject of where I was last night, hoping she'll hold on for the ride.

She doesn't. "You were with a man, weren't you?"

I nod as my hand jumps to my chin.

"Maybe I can meet him sometime?" She tilts her face forward. "Is he someone I should meet?"

You have no idea, Alexa. You have no fucking idea.

"You'll meet him," I say with every confidence. "I know you will."

"Good." She turns on her heel. "I'll tell Noah we're going to your place."

***

I plow through my day, listening to Vivian's incessant ramblings about what happened on the latest episode of a crime drama that hasn't seen a production schedule in more than a decade. I should really tell her to Google that entire episode guide to save her the endless hours she'll stay glued to her laptop, watching a handsome, fit detective solve a crime, without any strings attached, in less than an hour.

"Were you seriously hurt?"

I turn abruptly to face the voice asking the almost-too-personal question. "I'm fine."

It's Vivian. The concern in her tone is masking the unusually high lilt in her voice. "I was worried when a doctor called."

"I was concerned about missing work," I offer in response. "I wanted to be here. I'm sorry I couldn't be."

"I'm shocked you're here today." She takes a step closer to me and I swear I see actual compassion in her eyes. "It sounds like it was a pretty hard fall."

"I'm clumsy," I chuckle. "I need to get better at walking in heels."

"He sounded nice," she begins before she takes a short breath. "I mean the doctor that called about you, he sounded really nice."

"He was helpful." My words are clipped. I don't want to delve into the personal details of my relationship with Ben.

She taps her hand on the edge of my desk. "Is he accepting new patients?"

I purse my lips together. I have to wonder if she's asking because she's nursing a pain or a stubborn cough that won't go away or if her interest in Ben falls beyond the scope of what he can offer in his office. "I have no idea."

"What's his name again?" She skims her finger across the screen of her smart phone.

"Dr. Foster," I say slowly. "His name is Dr. Ben Foster."

She taps something into her phone before she turns to walk away. "Thanks, Kayla. I'll give him a call."

As I watch her walk away my mind instantly wanders to thoughts about how many other women search Ben out to find out exactly how thorough his bedside manner is.

Chapter 12

"How often do you fuck your patients?" The words sound less hostile coming out through a moan. This isn't the time to talk about this. I shouldn't be thinking of any other woman. I shouldn't be…

"Kayla," he spits my name out between heavy thrusts. "I'm fucking you."

He is fucking me. It's hard and slow. I'm on my back, his large frame hovering above me as he leisurely slides his cock into me, over and over again.

"Harder," I beg.

The friction is pushing me to the edge quickly. He ate me as soon as I let him into my apartment. He was on his knees, my back splayed against the door, my skirt a twisted mess around my waist as he buried his tongue inside of me, pulling my lust from within, pouring it onto his tongue.

"You're so tight." He growls the words into my neck. His tongue is tearing a path across my flesh. "Your cunt is so wet."

My hips buck involuntarily at the words. He's so direct and uninhibited. His body owns his pleasure and he's not afraid to take what he wants. I've never been with a man who is so commanding in bed. I've never felt my desire heightened to this extreme. This is a man made to fuck women, hard and senseless.

"I'm going to come again," I spit the words out into his shoulder. "It feels too good."

"It's so good." He pumps harder. His cock plunges deep with each lunge.

I cry out as I feel my body tense. I hold steady to his shoulders, knowing that if I let go, my body will betray me. I'll flail helplessly. I won't be able to control its instinctive reaction. I'll be lost and I'll miss my chance to enjoy his release.

He watches my face intently as I come. His lips part slightly, his tongue darts over them. "You're so beautiful when you come."

I stare at him, challenging him with a deep movement of my hips. "Come, Ben."

"Not yet." The movement of his head mirrors his words. "I don't want it to end."

I push harder, grinding my heels into the bed. "I've never been fucked like this before."

His eyes widen, his breathing stalls and he drops a litany of curse words from his lips as he pumps his hips into me.

***

"What kind of a doctor are you?" I pull the sheet over my breasts as I watch him toss the condom in a wastebasket in the corner of my bedroom.

He turns his head sharply; the grin on his face is disarming. "A very good one."

I don't doubt that. He has a compassionate edge to him that I haven't noticed in Noah. I have seen small flashes of concern in his gestures and the way he cares for Alexa, but Noah has built walls around himself emotionally because of the stabbing. Ben doesn't have those same restraints. I don't push the issue. It's not pressing on my mind like other questions are right now. "When will you talk to Noah?"

"I thought we were talking about me." His tone is teasing in an abstract way. He's preoccupied. I can sense it by the way he's reaching for his smartphone.

"I want to talk about Noah." I need to talk about Noah. I want to understand what happened between the two of them that was so significant it fractured their bond. "I'd like to understand your relationship with him."

He turns to face me now, his hand dropping to his hip. "It's very complicated, Kayla."

"He used the same word to describe it." I pull my knees to my chest, wrapping the sheet around me. "Noah said it was complicated too."

His brow peaks slightly at the admission. "What else has he said about me?"

It's a question typically reserved for teenage girls when they have their eye on a boy who will only share his feelings through a friend. "Noah doesn't talk about you."

I can't gauge his reaction. He throws his eyes to the floor to mask whatever emotion might be there. "I don't like talking about him either."

He's looking for an out. He came here to fuck me with the hope that I'd forget the reason I initially called him over. "I can't keep this from Alexa much longer."

The '*this*' I'm referring to isn't singular. It's not solely about the fact that I'm sleeping with Ben. It's not exclusively centered on my knowledge of who Noah's brother is and the fact that he lives only a few blocks from them. It's the entire fucked up scenario. I just had amazing sex with Noah Foster's twin brother. I ache inside to be near him when I'm not. I'm falling for him and whether that's my heart's way of masking the pain of Parker's rejection or it's genuine and is coming from a place of purity, it's my truth. My life is fucked up. My heart is twisting about in my chest and the only person I can talk to it about is the man at the center of my emotional hurricane.

"It won't be much longer." It's a classic technique meant to stall me. He doesn't offer anything to back it up. His eyes dart to the screen of his smartphone again.

Ultimatums have no place in the bedroom unless I've been denied an orgasm. In that case I'll use them to my full advantage, but now, with my mind in such a tortured place, I'm going to pull one out and shoot it at him.

"If you don't talk to Noah soon about us, I will." There's not a drop of hesitation in the words. There can't be. I'm serious.

He drops his phone on the dresser before walking to stand next to the bed. "It's not as cut and dry as that, Kayla. He believes things about me that aren't true. He'll turn you against me."

"He can't." My voice is insistent. "There's nothing that Noah can tell me that will change what I'm feeling."

"What are you feeling?" His hand scrubs the back of his neck. The nervous energy that surrounds him is palpable.

"I like you," I offer.

He pinches his fingers together on the bridge of his nose. "I like you too, Kayla. I really like you."

I smile at the confession. "I'd like to see you more often."

"I want to see you every day," he says in a low voice. "I actually want to see you every moment of every day. I wish that I could."

"It's so strange that I met your family before I met you. Do you talk to your father?" I throw the question out as bait. I want to show him that I'm already connected to his family in a roundabout way. Smoothing over the issues between him and Noah is inevitable, given the budding connection between us. Alexa is an integral part of my life, just as I'm an integral part of hers.

"My father?" He parrots back with a furrowed brow. "Do you know my father?"

"I've met him." Once. It was a few months ago at Noah's thirtieth birthday party. His father was brilliant, bold and very charismatic. I remember thinking that if my mother was single; Ron Foster would be the perfect fit for her. Now, the thought borders on uncomfortable.

"When? Where?" The questions rush out on top of one another.

"On Noah's birthday," I begin. "Wait. That was your birthday too."

He closes his eyes. A heavy breath draws his muscular chest up. "My father and Noah have a special bond."

It's an opening to something more. "What do you mean?" I inch sideways on the bed. It's a silent invitation for Ben to sit next to me. He doesn't move.

He teeters back on his heel. "He's closer to Noah than he is to me."

I'm getting nowhere. We're traveling in a circle that keeps leading us back to exactly the same place. "Ben, I've never had issues with my family." I haven't. When I was younger the disagreements were brief and forgotten easily.

"You're lucky."

"I know," I offer. "Alexa is part of my family though. She's like a sister to me."

He sits on the edge of the bed now, his thigh moving quickly up and down as his foot taps the floor. His cock dangles there, adrift in the space between his legs. "You're asking a lot of me."

The words sting even if their intention was something softer. He's going to turn this on me. He's going to tell me I'm pushing him into something he's not ready for. I hear it. I hear it beneath the rhythmic strumming of his heel against the hardwood floor. I see it in his shoulders, the way they're set forward and tense.

"I'm not. I'm telling you that if we continue to see each other I can't hide who you are from them. I'm asking you to talk to him and explain our relationship."

"What if I don't?" It's a challenge. His eyes don't engage me at all. He's staring straight ahead. I doubt he's focused on anything but the next words that will leave my lips.

"I'll talk to Alexa. She'll tell him."

He lets out a heavy sigh. His head drops to his hands. "This is so fucked up."

I reach for him, as much to quell the anxiety I see in his stance as to quiet my own shaking heart. I feel trapped in the middle of a family feud when I should be watching it from the sidelines. This is Alexa's family. These men make up the fabric of her future children's history. They are both a part of who her family will become. I didn't want this. No one would ask to be part of this willingly.

He recoils the instant my fingers brush against his knee. He's on his feet, his hands reaching wildly for his clothing. His boxer briefs are on in a flash. The pants he was wearing when he arrived are pulled back on and buttoned in haste. The shirt that he slung over the back of a wooden chair in the corner is now over his shoulders. "I can't..."

He can't. He can't what. What the fuck can't he do?

I want to jump to my feet and stop him. I should. I feel connected to him in ways I haven't felt with a man before. This is different. He's not the same as anyone I've ever known.

"I need to go. I'm sorry."

Parker. Those are Parker's words. He said those exact words to me as he packed up a suitcase and slammed it shut with a loud finality before he ran out of my life and into the night.

"Go," I say without thought. The words come from inside of me. "Just go."

I won't get on my knees and beg for a man to stay again. I won't sacrifice myself for a brief reprieve from the pain. He's leaving. I'll let him. Whatever this was, it's over now too.

Chapter 13

"Alexa says you're thinking about going for your master's degree."

I turn to stare at him in the doorway of the bedroom. He's wearing jeans that are slung low on his hips and a t-shirt. The tattoos that cover his arms are a bright contrast to the stark white of the shirt.

"It's a thought." I smile at him. "If I stay at my job for six months they offer some incentives for school."

Noah nods and a small grin pulls at the corner of his mouth. "Alexa is really proud of you. I am too."

It's a compliment I couldn't have seen coming. I came over in the middle of the day with the hope that I'd avoid them both. I'm still struggling with what to do. Ben has texted me repeatedly all week asking for my forgiveness, wanting to talk to me. I've thrown myself full force into my work and a plan to grab the future I want, without a man attached to it. Pursuing my master's degree was all I spoke about with Alexa when we had lunch two days ago. It wasn't only to get her opinion on my new plan to reclaim my life. It was to avoid bringing up the subject of Ben. A small part of me was still hoping, beyond hope, that he'd reach out to Noah.

"Do you need me to help you carry the rest of your things?" He nods towards the small cardboard box I'd packed full with the rest of my clothes.

"I can handle it." I arch my arm to show him my non-existent bicep muscle. "I may not have guns like you but I can get the job done."

"Guns?" He mirrors my pose and it's impressive. His body is almost identical in size and stature to his brother's.

"Can I talk to you about something, Noah?" It's hard for me to find the words from within but this may be my chance to gain a better understanding of Ben's reluctance to reach out.

"Anything." He pulls on the fabric of his jeans, giving him more room to sit on the edge of the bed.

I'm standing directly across from him. "It's about your brother."

His head pops up, the scar that transverses his cheek moves slightly as his jaw tenses. "Was Alexa talking about him again?"

"No." My hands tighten together in a knotted mess. "She hasn't brought it up at all."

I can't tell whether he believes me or if the words are being construed as my trying to protect my best friend. "Why are you asking then?" he asks in a low growl.

He's intimidating. The tattoos and scar make him appear more menacing than he is. I've heard about the kindness in his heart from Lex. I've seen the way he treats her. He loves her more than anything.

I scratch my neck. "It's just that. Well, I..." I stammer.

"I don't like talking about him."

I pinch my lips together before I race my tongue over the bottom one. "I met him, Noah."

His hand reaches for the edge of the bed. He grabs hold of it and it's hard to tell if he's steadying himself against the wall of emotions that have hit him full force or if he's questioning whether he heard me correctly. "You met Ben?"

I'd imagined that moment when Ben's name would come out of Noah. Alexa has never offered his name when she speaks about him and I've always assumed it's because she doesn't know it. He's only ever been Noah's twin brother when she's discussed him with me. "Yes."

His eyes meet mine. "When?"

This is the point when I have to decide if I'll tell him about the first night. I'm ashamed that I crawled into the bed of a man I just met. I'm confused that the man turned out to be his brother. A brother who obviously caused him immeasurable pain based on his reaction to my confession now.

"Christ, Kayla." He jumps to his feet, his large frame looming over me. "Did you meet him at the hospital? It wasn't when you fell and cracked your forehead a couple of weeks ago, was it?"

I rub the wound on my head. It's almost healed completely now. The only lingering reminder is dull flashes of pain from time-to-time. "He helped me that night."

He runs his hands over his face. "I knew this would happen eventually."

"What?"

"That someone would end up in the ER and see him there. Have you told Alexa?" His hands jump to my shoulders.

I shake my head slowly. "I wouldn't do that. I wanted to tell you first."

He nods before he pulls me into an unexpected embrace. "Don't talk to her about him. She'll go down to the hospital and find him. That can't happen."

I pull back to look at his face. "Why not?"

"It's best this way." He takes a step back, his dark eyes catching mine. "He's done horrible things. He's hurt people."

"What people?" I push. "What did he do?"

"It doesn't matter anymore." He turns to walk out of the room. "Stay away from him, Kayla. Stay as far away from him as you can."

Chapter 14

"Is Dr. Foster working?" Yes, that's right. I do not know how to listen when it concerns my own well-being. Everything Noah said to me has gone through my own personal filter and I've come to the conclusion that I need to know what the fuck is going on.

The woman behind the bustling information desk taps a few keys on her computer keyboard. "He's here. He's working in ER. It's that way." Her finger juts past me towards double doors.

"I know the way," I say back to her even though she's now barking an order to someone on the other end of a phone call.

I step through the doors into a world that is chock-full of noise, dozens of people sitting in an overcrowded waiting room and hospital staff milling about.

I know enough to not ask the women at the desk about Ben. I can tell by the crowd of people gathered in front of them that their hands are full. I came here to see him. I'll wait until he has a moment.

"Kayla?" His voice calls from the left as if on cue. "What's wrong?"

He's beside me in an instant, his hand flying to my hairline. "Is it your head? Are you still experiencing headaches?"

I stare at him, soaking in the image of him in a lab coat, a stethoscope strung loosely around his neck. I've never seen him like this. The night I was in the ER he was still dressed in jeans and a sweater. Now, he officially looks like a doctor. Where is the horrible person that Noah talked about? How can a man who has devoted his life to helping people heal be as bad as Noah says he is? "No, it's fine."

"Are you sick?" He motions behind me towards a nurse. "Let's get you into a room."

"I'm not sick." I lean closer to him. "That's not why I'm here."

He holds his hand up to stop a woman who is throwing numbers at him at breakneck speed. "I'm busy, Lynette. I'll be there shortly."

The huff that escapes her lips is audile. "We're very busy, Dr. Foster. Make it quick."

My eyes bolt to the side to her face. She's frustrated with his dismissal. She doesn't make eye contact with me at all.

"Give me a moment, I said." Ben's eyes don't leave mine. "This is important."

"Fine," she bites the word out in a hiss. It's obvious by her tone that it's anything but fine.

"Ben," I whisper his name quietly for no reason than to temper everything I'm feeling. "You shouldn't have walked out on me the other night."

"Christ, I was an idiot about that." His hand clenches in a fist on his chest. "It wasn't right. I can't tell you how sorry I am. I panicked when you were talking about Noah."

"I talked to him about you."

His jaw tenses slightly. It shifts the structure of his face and a glimpse of Noah is there for an instant. "You told him I was your lover?"

I feel the word roar with full force to my core. Lovers? We haven't defined it. I hadn't. Ben had, obviously. "No. I just told him that I met you."

He nods his head slightly. "What did he say?"

"He knew you worked here." I point to the floor. "I told him you helped me when I got hurt."

He leans forward slightly, pivoting on his shoe. "He told you to stay away from me, didn't he?"

I nod. "I want to know why."

He pulls on the collar of his lab coat, adjusting it slightly. "I should be off by eleven but it's never that simple." His hand drifts towards the waiting room.

"I understand," I say wishing that he could just walk away from his responsibilities here for an hour so he could explain to me what happened between him and his brother. My entire being is telling me that the issue isn't as serious as Noah has made it out to be. I've been with Ben. I've felt the tenderness in his touch. I've been nursed back to health by him. I don't see the evil that lives beneath the surface that Noah claims is there.

His name wafts through the air over the public announcement system.

"I need to go." His lips brush against mine in a gentle kiss. "I'll text you when I'm done here."

He grazes past me in his rush to help others. Right now, at this very moment in time, I wish I was the one he was helping.

Chapter 15

"I can't begin to imagine what Noah told you about me." He pulls off his suit jacket to lower himself into a seat across from me in a bustling mid-town bistro.

When Ben had called me late last night, I'd been wary of letting him come over. It wasn't out of fear for my personal safety. It was out of the clear knowledge that I'd want him. Noah's warnings hadn't crushed my desire for Ben at all. The only thing that had done that was his need to rush out of my apartment the other day when he felt cornered.

"Did you order something to eat?" His eyes scan the expansive menu.

I study his face briefly, marveling in how strong his features are. I know that he's not Noah's identical twin but there's no mistaking they're brothers. I wonder what it would be like seeing them standing side-by-side. "I'm not that hungry."

"We can split a sandwich." He motions towards a waitress standing near the cash register.

I sit in silence while he orders our lunch. My hands are sweating. Even though Alexa still knows nothing about Ben, I can't help but feel I'm betraying her. I spoke to her briefly on the phone this morning about having dinner together tonight. I'd balked at making firm plans because I wanted to see how my lunch with Ben would go.

"Tell me about Noah." He leans back in the wooden chair. "It starts with him telling you to avoid me at all costs, right?"

The sarcasm dripping from each of the words is measurable. I can see the disdain in his expression. He disapproves of Noah too, but it's not the same. Ben's never warned me away from his brother. "He did say that, yes."

"Did he say why?" He picks up a small glass of room temperature water that the waitress dropped off when she took his order.

I sigh deeply. "No, Ben. He wouldn't say why."

"You want to know why?" He sips a mouthful before resting the glass back down.

I do, don't I? That's why I'm here. I stare at him while I contemplate the gravity of the question. I don't really need to do this. I can get up, walk out and never look back. Ben Foster can become a distant memory and the secret of his silent feud with Noah can rest in peace. That would be the right thing to do. That would be the way to honor my friendship with Alexa and the man she loves.

"It started when our mother died."

The words are almost emotionless. His expression doesn't add anything to it either. They're just words that he's pushed out at me and now, I have to absorb them. Is that because he's a doctor and death is a natural part of his everyday life now?

"When did she die?"

"It's feels like a lifetime ago now." His long fingers tap a beat against the table. "It feels like yesterday."

"You were close." I know the assumption is based on the fact that he told me that Noah and his father shared a special bond. Maybe Ben loved his mother the same way. Maybe he was the shining light in her eyes.

"I took care of my mother." His eyes are empty. "I wanted to be a doctor because of her."

I smile at the knowledge. "She must have been lovely."

"She was beautiful and kind." His hand jumps to his chest. "She was sweet. She loved me very much."

"What happened to her?"

"She was ill for weeks before her death." His eyes dart up but move past me quickly, centering on a spot in the diner behind me. "The doctors said it was a virus. They sent her home."

"It wasn't a virus?" I don't know what else to ask. I have no inkling of what it means or how it impacted her health. I have no baseline to judge by.

His eyes travel the path of the waitress as she drops off our lunch. I watch in silence as he takes a healthy bite of the sandwich. He motions for me to dig in, but I can't eat. I'm slightly miffed that he can considering the fact that we are embroiled in a serious discussion about someone he loved.

He watches me intently as he chews. No words are spoken between us. The conversation ended in the exact place I need and want it to continue so I wait patiently until he clears the entire plate.

"Kayla." He finally speaks. "This is very hard to talk about."

I nod. I know that it is. I want to hear it though. I need to understand the nucleus of his pain. "I know," I say quietly. "I care about you, Ben."

A trace of a smile forms on his lips. "I care about you too."

"What happened when she died?" I ask out of sheer need. I'm nauseous from the anxiety that is racing through me.

His eyes dart down to his lap. "She needed care around the clock. My father, Noah and I all took turns with her."

I can't imagine the pain that seeps into those who have to watch someone they love wither away like that. "That must have been very hard."

"The alternative was the hospital. She didn't want that."

"I understand." I'm trying to understand. I still don't have a clear idea of when any of this happened. The emotional strength of a fifteen-year-old boy is obviously much different than a twenty-five-year old. Judging by the depth of the fracture in Ben's family, I'm guessing she died when the twins were much younger.

"I was watching her the day that she died." He pushes his water glass aside so he can reach across the table for my hand. "I had a friend over."

He doesn't need to elaborate. It was a woman, or girl. The thoughtful gesture to hold my hand is telling me that.

"We were in the guest house when it happened."

I nod. I pull my free hand to my forehead. I'm uncomfortable hearing the pointed details now. I pushed for this. I need to accept it.

"My father and Noah were at a ball game. By the time they got home, she'd been gone for hours."

"You didn't call them to tell them?" I ask the question without any thought. It just rolls off my tongue.

"I didn't know." His eyes stare into mine. I see the emptiness in them. "I was in the guest house, fucking some woman whose name I can't recall over and over again while my mother took her very last breath."

Chapter 16

"You have a secret." Alexa pulls on my ponytail from behind.

I almost choke on the mouthful of wine I'm trying to swallow. "What secret?" It's not a random question. When it comes to secrets, I'm hiding more than one.

"You're seeing someone, aren't you?"

"Seeing as in dating?" Nice stall tactic, Kayla. You really expect that's going to work?

She scowls as she takes a seat beside me on the weathered couch in my apartment. "Call it whatever you like. There's a man in your life."

"Why would you ask me that?" I try to level my voice. I haven't seen Ben since the diner but that means little in the big picture. I'm still sorting through my feelings. I'm debating whether or not to talk to Noah. I feel torn between my friendship to him and Lex and my attraction to Ben.

"There's a man's tie hanging from the towel rack in your bathroom." She tosses her head towards the hallway. "It's expensive too."

"How do you know if it's expensive," I scoff in an overly exaggerated attempt to change the subject. I knew that tie was there. I liked having it there as a reminder of Ben. Now it's pushing me into a corner.

"Noah just bought a new suit." She taps her hand on my thigh. "It was expensive. I saw that exact tie at the store. Noah almost bought it."

"Noah in a suit?" I struggle to conjure up that image. "He's not a suit kind of guy, is he?"

"He's a handsome kind of guy," she counters. "I like when he dresses up if we go out for dinner."

"Makes sense." I breathe a sigh of relief. If I can keep her on the subject of her fiancé, I'll keep her off the subject of the twin brother of her fiancé.

"It was nice to see him spend some money on himself." She takes a large drink from her wineglass. "He's going to get a tux for the wedding."

I smile at the joy in her voice when she talks about her wedding. "It's coming up soon."

"We're signing a pre nup next week."

"You're signing a pre nup?" It's not that surprising given how successful Noah is. He used to sell the nude photographs he took of women for tens of thousands of dollars. That has to add up quickly.

"It was my idea." She shrugs her shoulders. "He's worth a lot of money."

"He sold a lot of photographs back in the day," I tease. We don't talk about Noah's former career much anymore. It's never been a sore spot for Alexa. She posed for him too at one point.

"He got a huge inheritance when he turned twenty-five." Her words are slightly slurred. "It was from when his mother died."

I know more about that event than I should. "I guess a pre nup is a good idea then." I can't think of anything else to say.

"Do you want to know something?" She swallows the last bit of wine that had settled at the bottom of the glass. "It's about his brother."

Hell, yes, I want to know.

I nod only slightly.

"I think Noah hates him because of that money." She runs her finger along the edge of the glass. "He got some money too."

"Why would you think that?"

"I heard him talking to Ron about it on the phone." She's whispering so loud that I'm certain anyone passing by on the street would hear every single word she's said.

I had wondered how Ben could afford his apartment and wardrobe on an ER doctor's salary. "Sometimes money makes people crazy." I spin my finger in the air. "I'm sure their problems go deeper than that."

"I don't know about that." She starts to stand before falling back into the soft cushion of the couch. "Noah hates Ben. If it's not the money it has to be a woman."

It is a woman. It's the woman who gave them life. The very same woman whose death pulled them apart for good.

Chapter 17

"Get the fuck in here." He pulls on my hand sending me flying into his apartment. I hear the door slam shut behind me.

"Ben," I mutter his name in a heated rush before his lips bear down on mine. "I…Ben…" I try to form the words through his kiss but he's too aggressive.

"I've been thinking about you for days." His hands are pulling on the tie of my wraparound dress, tangling me up in it. "I'm going to rip this fucking thing off your body."

I take a step back as much to save my dress as to calm my breath. "I'll take it off."

His eyes are glued to my hands as he strips off his own clothes, throwing them onto the floor in a pile.

"Look how hard you make me." His hand runs fast over his thick, erect cock. "I need to be inside that sweet cunt of yours now."

The words fill me with an instant hunger that I can't quench. I've tried to wean myself off of him by touching myself in my bed. I thought that would quiet the desperate need I've been feeling. I want him so much. I can't keep denying it. I don't want to deny it. I want to own it and embrace it. When he called to tell me to come over, I hadn't hesitated at all. My need for him is primal and unending.

I pull my panties down and stand before him, completely naked and exposed. I'm not shy. I've never been one to hide my body beneath a sheet out of fear that my lover will find fault. I've never complained about the size of my breasts or the width of my hips. I love my body. He loves my body. I see it in his eyes and I feel it when he's making love to me.

"Goddamn, Kayla." He narrows the space between us with easy strides. His hands wrap around my sides, pulling me into him. His cock rests against my thigh, heavy, warm and eager.

I moan as he picks me up, pulling my legs around him. I cry out when he clears the desk near the door with one swoop of his hand and lowers my body onto it and I whimper as I watch him cloak his beautiful cock with a condom.

"I need you, Kayla." His breath whispers over my lips. "I've needed you since that first night."

I cling tightly to him as he enters me completely, his cock pushing me to my limits, stretching me wide with a bite of pain that touches my core. "Ben, yes," I moan into his mouth. "Fuck me."

He pulls my ass to the edge of the desk as he sits me up, our bodies still connected. "Look at me, Kayla. Look at me."

I open my eyes. His face is so beautiful. It's so perfect and kind. I stare into his eyes with my own as he fucks me with slow, easy, graceful strokes.

***

"If you tell them about me, I'll lose you." His voice pierces through the darkness in the room.

I shake myself awake. I'd drifted off after he'd carried me to his bed and fucked me again. "That won't happen," I whisper into the empty space before me.

His hands pull me closer so my back is resting against his chest. "It will. Noah won't let her talk to you anymore."

The concept is foreign. Noah wouldn't demand anything that restricting of Lex. Our relationship is close, too close for a brotherly feud to tear it apart. "Alexa would never stop talking to me."

"He'll fill her head with lies about me." His voice is shaky and uncertain.

I try to flip over. I want to look at him when he tells me this. These people are the core of my inner circle. They are my New York family. I need them as much as I need air to breathe. I can't lose Alexa. I won't.

"Alexa is smarter than that," I say with every effort to sound convincing. "She won't break off our friendship over this."

"We should see where this goes before you tell her."

I know the words shouldn't burst open my heart the way they do. This is new and it's natural to have doubts. He's older than I am. He's wiser. Maybe when a person turns thirty they realize that banking on an undeniable connection is foolish and impulsive. I'm not thirty-years-old. He is. I want to fall into the well of promise. I want to revel in the idea that this has a future beyond a few more months of incredible sex.

"Or I could tell her and then we could see where it goes," I counter. Two can play wicked mind games, Dr. Foster.

"He blames me for our mother's death." His voice is dark. "That's never going to change, Kayla."

"You don't know that." I push his hands lower wanting to feel his fingers rush through my folds. "You can't predict that." I don't want to talk about Noah. I can't think about Alexa. All I want is Ben.

He gives in to my silent demands as his finger finds my clit. "I know that I'm not going to give this up for anything."

I spread my legs brazenly, kicking the sheet off of us. I reach down to cover his hand with my own. "You don't have to give this up."

He pushes a finger into me, luxuriously pulling the dampness from my channel before gliding it back over my clitoris. "You're mine. Noah can't take you away from me. No one can."

"No one can." I arch my back to give him more access. "No one will."

Chapter 18

"I saw you with him."

I know his voice before I turn to look at him. It's Noah.

"When?" It's not as though the details matter. I can hear the disappointment in his voice. There's no denying the anger that is sprinkled through his words. He's pissed.

"Yesterday." I sense movement behind me. "You were leaving his apartment and he kissed you in front of the building."

My focus was solely on Ben in that moment. He was hailing me a cab, sending me back home after he'd licked me to orgasm one last time. I'd felt treasured in that moment. He'd leaned down before shutting the taxi door to tell me he'd miss me.

"Why were you there?" I turn now to look at him. He's standing less than a foot away from me in a crowded bakery. "Why are you here now?"

"Alexa told me about the tie."

"What tie?" I take a step back. "I don't know what you're talking about."

"His tie was in your apartment."

The tie. That fucking tie that she saw in my bathroom. "It was just a tie, Noah."

He moves closer to me, his hand jumping to my elbow. "I went to buy a suit because Alexa asked me to."

"Yes," I say because there's nothing else to offer as he steers me through the crowd and onto the street.

We finally stop near the edge of the building. The pedestrian traffic is moving quickly just a few feet away from us.

"I wanted that tie until the sales woman told me that they'd only sold one like that." His eyes bore into me. "She thought it was amusing that it was sold to another Mr. Foster. Actually, she said Dr. Foster bought it."

You've got to be shitting me. I'm busted because of a goddamn necktie?

"You had no right to follow me to his place, Noah." I know the words sound petulant and spiteful. "I'm old enough to make my own decisions."

"Alexa loves you." He taps his hand on my shoulder. "You're like a sister to her."

I don't feel the guilt that is implied within the words. Why should I? "Alexa gets to love you, why can't I..."I stop myself. I don't love Ben. I'm crazy in like with Ben. "Why can't I be with Ben?"

"He's a no good piece of lying shit," he hisses each word slowly over his tongue. "He's not who you think he is."

"Maybe he's not who you think he is." I push my finger into his hard chest. "Maybe you just can't get over losing your mother."

He takes a step back as his hand reaches to the brick façade of the building. I hear him curse beneath his breath. "You don't know what you're talking about."

"I do." I take a step closer to him. I'm the one on the offense now. He doesn't get to dictate my life to me. That's not how this works.

His eyes search my face. "What did he tell you?"

It's common knowledge. It's not as though I'll be betraying Ben in any way if I repeat what he told me. "He said you and your father blame him for your mother's death."

"He actually told you that?" He doesn't hesitate as he barks the words at me. "I can't believe he told you that."

I stare at him. I can't gauge whether Noah's reaction is strictly based in the emotional void that he's felt since losing his mom or if he's harboring more resentment towards Ben than he's letting me see. "Noah," I say his name softly. "Ben told me he was with someone the day your mom died. He told me he was supposed to be watching her."

His brow furrows as he digests my words. "Say that again." He leans forward craning his ear towards me.

"Ben told me that he was in the guest house with a woman while you and Ron were out."

His hand flies in the air in a circular motion. "Go on."

I blow a heavy puff of air out between my lips. "He said that she died and he didn't know until you both came home."

His chin tilts down as his hand scrubs over his forehead. I've seen Ben do the very same thing. "That's what Ben told you?"

I nod slowly looking for confirmation of the story in Noah's eyes. I find nothing but a blank stare.

"Do you trust me, Kayla?"

It's not a fair question. If he asked me at any other moment in time I'd tell him absolutely without hesitation. Noah is an extension of Alexa in my eyes. I can count on him. I know he wants the best for me. The only problem is that in this instance, he can't see things clearly. His resentment and hatred for his brother is clouding his judgement.

"It's not that simple, Noah."

"It's a very simple question." He taps his fingers against the brick. "You are an incredibly important person to the woman I love. She needs you. She counts on you. I can't let anything happen to you."

I scratch the back of my ear. "Nothing bad is going to happen to me, Noah."

"He will hurt you." His voice is calm and controlled. "He will damage you in ways you can't even imagine. You are nothing to him. Nothing."

I lean back into the wall for balance. "Ben is a good person. He's a doctor."

He shakes his head slightly. "You think that makes him a saint?"

"No," I say briskly. "I'm not naïve, Noah. You're making me feel like an idiot."

"He didn't tell you everything about the day she died. I doubt he's told you everything about his life." The words bite into me deeply. He's making me feel silly and foolish for falling into bed with Ben.

"I'm not marrying him, Noah," I offer as a reprieve. "I'm just having fun with him."

He throws his head back in frustration. "I am trying desperately to protect you. Why can't you see that?"

"You are angry with him because your mother died." I reach for his forearm. "That doesn't make him a bad person."

"I am angry with him because he has fucked over every single person who was close to him, including me." His free hand jumps to cover mine. "He uses people as if they are nothing. He takes what he can from them and then throws them away like trash."

I shake my head. "That's wrong."

"It's right." He squeezes my hand harder. "He's a master at manipulating people. He tried to ruin my life. "

"How?" I shoot the question out without realizing how much desperation is attached to it.

He scrubs his hand over his face. "I can't talk to you about this, Kayla. I need to talk to Alexa first. It will kill her inside if she knows I'm sharing stuff about Ben with you and not her."

Normally, I'd take that as a weak excuse for wanting to hold his secrets close to him, but this is Noah Foster. Alexa is his life and I know that he honors her in a way few men honor the woman they adore.

"What am I supposed to do?" I ask genuinely. I feel completely conflicted inside. I have nothing concrete to dissuade me from Ben's confessions about the day his mother died. All I have to contradict that are some loosely disguised accusations that have come from my best friend's boyfriend.

"Stay away from him." He pushes on my hand. "I'm going home right not to tell Alexa everything about Ben. Then you'll come over and the three of us will talk about this together."

I nod. It's not in agreement. I want to know what happened in the past that has convinced Noah that Ben is the second coming of evil. I want to hear it from Ben. I need to talk to him now.

"Promise me you'll stay away from him."

That's not a promise I can keep. "I want to know what's really going on, Noah."

"You will." He reaches forward to graze his lips across my cheek. "I should have told Alexa about all this months ago. I'll talk to her and then we'll talk again."

I sigh deeply as he turns and heads down the street.

Chapter 19

"Have you ever wanted something that was bad for you?" I pull air quotes around the word *bad*. I don't know how else to define what Noah thinks of Ben.

"I'm a doctor." He laughs as his hand races up my thigh. "Everything is bad for me. There's like two things I should be eating. Everything else is the root cause of some kind of disease."

I laugh at the words even though I'm bundled into a tight ball inside. I keep glancing at my phone waiting for Noah or Alexa to call.

"Are you expecting a call?" Ben nods his chin towards my smartphone.

"I am." I've been debating whether I should just ask Ben about Noah's attack on his character. I trust them both. I care about them both. I feel as though I'm sitting atop a thick tug-of-war rope that they both are clinging to for dear life.

"Is it a work thing?" He moves his body closer to mine. "Your boss was in the ER the other day."

"What?" I ask in surprise even though I anticipated it happening at some point. "She was smitten with you that day you called in for me."

"Smitten?" he parrots back within a wide grin. "Is that like saying she's hot for me?"

"All your female patients are."

"Some of the male ones too, " he says through a wide grin.

"It's not about work. I'm waiting for Noah to call."

His jaw tenses at the mention of his brother's name. "Why would Noah be calling you?"

"He's talking to Alexa about a few things right now." I pick up my phone and hold it in my hand. "Then they'll call me so I can go over."

"What kind of things?" He leans back into the soft leather of his couch. "Wedding things?"

"No." This is it, Kayla. Just say it. "It's about you."

"Me?" His finger scoops a piece of hair behind my ear, before it floats down my cheek. "What about me?"

"Noah knows we're sleeping together."

"How does Noah know that?" He tilts his chin towards me. "You told Noah?"

"No." I shake my head. "He saw us together."

He leans forward to brush his lips against my cheek. "It's not the end of the world. You know he'll try and poison your mind with thoughts about how bad I am, don't you?"

I feel the rope pulling me closer to Ben. "He said you weren't good for me. He said you'd ruin me."

"Ruin you?" He smirks as he says the words. "How can I possibly ruin someone so completely perfect?"

They're words. They are simple words that melt hearts. "He said you tried to ruin his life."

His brow cocks. "Did he tell you how I did that?"

He's so calm. If anything Noah said was based in truth, wouldn't Ben be trying to convince me that Noah is a liar? I stare at his face. There's no panic or frustration. He's as collected now as when I arrived a few minutes ago.

I place my phone into my lap. "You'd tell me if there was more to your feud than what happened the day your mother died, right?"

"I told you, Kayla." He brushes his lips over my cheek. "Noah hates me because I let her die."

I turn my head slightly, catching his lips with mine. My hand floats to the back of his head, deepening the kiss. There's no possible way this beautiful, tender man would hurt me. It's not part of who he is. I've watched him in the moments when he thinks I'm not paying attention. I've seen the way he smiles at the people who pass us by on the street. He has dedicated himself to helping others regain their health. Noah is wrong. He can't possibly be right.

"I want to believe you so much," I say into the kiss. "I know you're a good person."

He nods as his lips race up my cheek to my forehead. "I've tried very hard to be someone my mother would be proud of."

I move my other arm to embrace him, pulling his tall frame into me. "Noah doesn't want me to be with you, Ben."

"I know." He wraps his arms tighter around me. "We'll figure it out. We're going to do that together."

A loud thump on the door stuns us both. He jumps from my embrace, his head jutting around the room. "I'm not expecting anyone."

I lean back waiting for him to get up. He doesn't move as another loud thud fills the space.

"You should get that." I push myself up. "Do you want me to get it?"

He reaches for my hand, pulling it to his mouth. "I'll get it. You wait here, okay?"

I stand in silence as I hear his shoes tap footsteps to the foyer. I can't see who it is but I hear the voice. It's loud. It's angry. It's Noah.

He rounds the corner with Alexa behind him. "Kayla, for Christ sake, what the fuck are you doing here?"

I'm stunned by the words. The strength of his anger pushes me back and onto the couch. I feel faint. Alexa is yelling at Ben. The words are all too quick and cluttered for me to make sense of them.

"Get the fuck out of here." Ben is in front of me now, shielding my body from them both. "I'll call the police. Get out."

"Kayla." Noah tries to dart around Ben but he holds him back. Their large frames are chest-to-chest now. "You have to come with us."

"No." I shake my head slightly. "Noah, please."

"Kayla," Alexa's voice calls from behind them both. I can hear her sobbing. "Oh God, Kayla."

I push myself up again. I need to stop this. They can't dictate my life like this.

"Ben." I tap him on his shoulder and he spins around instantly. "Let me talk to them. I'll tell them it's okay."

His eyes are filled with panic. His head twisting back to look at Noah. "Kayla, no." He grabs my hands, holding tightly to them. "Please, no."

"Leave." I look past him to where Noah is standing next to Alexa. "I'll come over right away so we can talk. Please leave."

"They arrested him, Kayla," Alexa screams through the air. "They arrested him after she died."

"Who?" My eyes sprint over Ben's face looking for an answer from him.

"Ben." Her hand flies past Noah. "Ben killed their mother."

"That's not true." I squeeze his hands, knowing the pain he must be in hearing those words. "Don't say that."

"He was charged with murder," Noah shouts at me. "He disconnected her oxygen, walked away and let her die."

My eyes travel up Ben's chest and then to his chin before they reach his face.

I stare at him.

"Ben." My voice is barely more than a whisper. "Tell me that's not true."

His lips part slightly, his hands jump to my face and within a sob he whispers the two words that change everything. "It's true."

RUIN

Part Two

Chapter 1

"Kayla, I didn't think you'd come."

"I couldn't stay away." It's a quick retort. The words are a clear reflection of the inner need that has been pushing against my better judgment for two days.

It's been two days since Noah and Alexa ripped wide open the wound that Ben has been nursing for the past twelve years. I watched in silence as he collapsed to his knees, his body wrought with sobs as Noah had stood over him, a litany of accusations pouring from his lips in a frenzied rush.

Even then, in that moment, I wanted to fall next to him, wrap him inside of my arms and shield him from the barrage of painful reminders of that day. I wanted to scream at Noah to back off. I wanted to force them to leave. I wanted time to stop just at the moment before Noah and Alexa knocked at the door.

"I'm sorry you were in the middle of that," he whispers, his eyes moving to the table next to us in the crowded hospital cafeteria. "I haven't seen Noah in years. Now you know why."

I don't really know why. I only know that Ben was arrested for his mother's death when he was a teenager. The blanks that need to be filled in are expansive and wide. I'd pulled Alexa and Noah out of Ben's apartment with the promise that I'd listen to all the facts. When we got back to their place, the details were sparse and disjointed. I left there only sure of one thing, that I needed to see Ben.

"Noah explained some of what happened." It's broad and meant to be open-ended. I don't know where to start. I have no bearing on where this conversation is supposed to begin.

He leans forward, resting his elbows on the table. "What did Noah tell you?"

"He didn't say much about the day." I meet his eyes. "He was upset."

In a range of understatements, that one is off the scale. Noah had ranted for more than an hour after leaving Ben's the other night. The words were heavy with anger and distrust. He had rattled on about loss, about life insurance, about trust. Alexa and I had sat, huddled in the corner, listening, waiting, wanting him to calm enough so that we could string together what had happened. I left their home with nothing more than deep regret. I had abandoned Ben on the floor to save him from Noah's ripe temper. I wished, almost instantaneously, that I had stayed and held him.

His thumb traces over the face of his watch, his eyes following its path. "He'll never forgive me for that day."

Forgiveness is a heady beast when death is on the table. They both loved their mother. I had heard it in the words Ben spoke days ago when he retraced the steps he took right before she died. I had seen it in Noah's face, and in his clenched fists, when he confessed to all the pain he's endured since that day.

I have nothing to offer that will change Ben's perception of his brother, other than the truth. "Noah is very angry. He's focused on the fact that you were arrested."

I am too. I haven't admitted it but there are some things that aren't easily ignored. This isn't a typical family squabble. Ben was arrested for his mother's death. He admitted it just days ago and that confession had been on constant replay in my mind.

"I was arrested." He leans closer, the words soft and low. "The charges were dropped almost immediately."

I should feel instant relief at that but it does little to quell the aching need I have inside of me to understand. I've tried to make sense of my inability to listen to Alexa and Noah and forget Ben. I'm smart enough to recognize that part of it is tied to my connection to Alexa. I held her trembling hand in mine as her fiancé paced the floor of their apartment, cursing the fact that he has a twin brother. She had embraced me before I left their place, whispering in my ear how she wished it were different.

The draw towards Ben is more than that though. It's not about the moments in his bed or the rush when I'm in his arms. It's in the person I see when I look in his eyes. There's tenderness and compassion there. It's been there since he first sat down next to me on the airplane.

"Why were you charged in the first place?" I ask. "How did that happen?"

He pushes the, now empty, paper coffee cup away from him and focuses his gaze on me. "It's very complicated, Kayla. I can't answer that here."

Here, being the hospital cafeteria. It's a place where people often gather to discuss death, or at the very least, the possibility of it. It's filled with muted whispers of doctors discussing patients, and patients discussing doctors and visitors trying to convince themselves that a five minute visit with a loved one in intensive care is better than no visit at all.

"When can we talk about it?" I ask bluntly. My need to know more isn't going to vanish now that I've looked at his face. My curiosity is piqued. The broken man that I left on the floor of his apartment two nights ago is now composed, calm and completely in control of our conversation.

"I'm working a split shift." His eyes flit past his watch again. "Can you come to my place tomorrow night?"

I nod. There's no way he can sense the bitter disappointment I'm feeling. I came here because of the bait of an explanation within his text message. I now realize it was a way for him to gauge my interest.

"It might be best if you didn't mention our meeting to Noah or Alexa."

"They are my family." The words leave my lips before I realize the irony woven into them. "I'm not hiding this from them."

He sucks in a deep breath as he pulls his tall frame from the plastic chair. "Understood. I'll have a car pick you up at eight."

Chapter 2

"When did you know he was Noah's brother?" She brushes a few loose strands of her hair away from her face. "I've been meaning to ask you that."

It's a question I've seen coming for days. We haven't discussed Ben at all up to this point. We've been avoiding the subject with effortless ease, allowing the events of the other night to settle before we dove back into the brunt of it all. "I didn't know who he was when I first met him. I realized when I fell on the sidewalk grate and he was the doctor helping me."

"You met him before you fell?" Her hand leaps to her neck, pulling on the pendant she's wearing. "When did you first meet him?"

I glance down to my lap briefly. "It was when I came back to New York. We were on the same flight."

"You mean a few weeks ago? When you moved back here after Parker left you?"

The reminder of Parker's abandonment doesn't sting anymore. I don't lurch at the mention of his name. "It was that night, yes."

"Night?" She takes a deep breath. "What do you mean night? You arrived in the morning."

It was a lie of omission. Alexa had no warning when I showed up on her doorstep that day. I hadn't corrected her when she scolded me for not calling her from the airport to come get me. I chose to let her believe that her apartment was my first, and only, stop when I touched down in New York City. "No. I arrived the night before."

"Where were you? Why didn't you come to my place?"

I want her to put the pieces of that puzzle together herself. I'm not worried about her condemning me for leaving the airport with someone I didn't know. Alexa and I have never judged one another in that way. If it was any other man, she'd probe me for details and congratulate me for taking a step towards forgetting Parker, but this is Ben. He's the one man her fiancé can't stand the sight of.

"I was with him." I pull in a deep breath. "I was with Ben that night."

"What?" Her tone is loud enough to draw glances from those seated near us in the café. "You slept with Ben that night?"

I pull my hands through my hair, separating the dark strands. "I didn't know his last name, Lex. We met on the plane and decided to hook up."

"You expect me to believe you didn't know he was Noah's brother?"

I expect her to believe that I'm being honest and open about what happened. "I didn't know."

"They look alike." She leans back in the chair, crossing her arms over her chest. "I saw the resemblance as soon as Ben opened the door the other night."

I stare at her, absorbing her words. "You saw the resemblance because you live with Noah. I'd only met Noah a handful of times before I left for Boston."

She closes her eyes and throws her head back. It's a classic sign of frustration. I've seen it enough to recognize it. "Kayla. I can't believe you didn't see Noah in him."

"Why would I see Noah in him?" I tap my fingers on the table. "No one ever told me Noah had a brother."

She blows a puff of air out between us. "He didn't want me to talk about it."

I nod, savoring a brief victory within the conversation. "I couldn't have known he was related to Noah. I had no idea."

"That's irrelevant." Her lips thin. "As soon as you knew, you should have told me."

"You're right," I acquiesce. "I should have."

Her face softens. "I'm just glad it's over now. None of us ever have to see him again."

This is the point where I confess. This is the point where I watch her face twist into a confused mess as she tries to process my unexplainable need to get Ben's side of the story. I promised myself I wouldn't sneak around behind her back. I don't want to be that friend. "Alexa, I…"

She cuts me off. "I'm supposed to meet Noah at the florist in ten minutes. Do you want to come?"

"You're choosing flowers for the wedding?" The concept shouldn't feel as absolutely foreign as it does to me. They're moving on a forward path towards marriage. Their reality is still intact.

She's on her feet. "I have to get my order in this week. You're welcome to come if you want."

The subtle difference between wanting me there and accepting my presence as a tag-along isn't lost on me. "I can't." I straighten my back in the chair. "I have a few things to take care of."

Her eyes don't leave her phone. "I'll text you tomorrow."

I nod. By this time tomorrow I'll have Ben's side of the tangled story that is tearing him and his brother apart.

Chapter 3

"I didn't kill my mother."

It's a confession that meets me just as I step over the threshold into his apartment. You'd think I'd have a response sitting ready on my tongue. I've thought about this conversation for more than a day. I've wondered what it would feel like to hear him tell me that he didn't do it. I want to hear it. If I'm being completely honest with myself, I need to.

"People jumped to conclusions." He reaches to grab my sweater and purse from my hands. "Noah jumped to conclusions."

I swallow hard. "Noah is very set in his beliefs about that day."

His gaze narrows. "I guess I can't blame you for believing what Noah says. You've known him longer than you've known me."

"I didn't say I believe Noah." My jaw tightens. "I said he has his own idea of what happened."

Turning his head, his eyes catch mine. "I want you to form your own conclusions. I want to give you the facts."

It's more than Noah has offered me. The other night, after we'd left this apartment, Noah hadn't responded to any of my questions. They had floated past him as he repeated over and over again that the reason his mother wasn't going to be at the wedding was because Ben had taken her from him. He spoke of the children he hopes to have with Alexa and how their grandmother will never cradle them or sing to them. Every path that his life has taken, or will take, has been immeasurably impacted by her death and the clear field of blame rests on Ben's shoulders.

"Do you want some wine?" His breath travels over my shoulder as we enter the main room. My eyes stop on the couch where I was sitting when Noah and Alexa barged in. They had come to pull me from Ben's clutches because they believed they knew what was best for me. They don't. They can't. I can't even say for certain that I know at this point.

"I'm fine," I say the words quietly, hoping that they're intent will rub off on me. I'm far from fine. I'm shaking inside.

He motions for me to sit. "I'll pass too then."

I turn my head to look at him as he lowers himself next to me. "I know it's not easy to talk about."

"It's not." He rubs his index finger over his right eyebrow. "I never talk about it but I want you to understand what happened."

The suggestion that it's important to him that I hear his truth quiets my racing heart. "You told me before that you were preoccupied when she died."

"I was with a woman," he says the words I was avoiding. "She was someone I met at a party the night before."

"I remember you telling me about her." I pause before I continue, "I know the details are fuzzy. It was a long time ago."

"I think I blocked out most of it because of what happened that day." His gaze is across the room, floating in the air. "I've thought about it since we first talked about it. Her name was Samantha, I think. She was older than me by a year or two. I remember that."

I lean forward resting my forearms against my legs. "That's the woman you took to the guesthouse?"

"It was my first time." His voice is closer than it was. "I'd never been with anyone before."

I can't say that this falls within the scope of what I expected to hear today. It's caught me so off guard that I feel as though I've lost my center. Ben is the most skilled lover I've had. He's been able to read the subtle nuances of my body as I near my release. He's taken control of my pleasure in a way that no man has ever done before. It's remote to hear him mention his first experience.

"I didn't know that," I offer unnecessarily. Of course I didn't know. We've never discussed our sexual pasts.

"I was impatient." A deep chuckle escapes him. "I was practically clawing at her clothes the moment she arrived."

I smile at the recollection. He was a young man with no experience who was presented an opportunity he'd likely been longing for. "I bet she was doing the same."

"I was tall and thin back then. I was very geeky." He adjusts himself next to me, crossing one long leg over another. "It was a wonder she even noticed me at all."

He's not looking for a compliment. It's not that he wants me to dissuade him from feeling that way but I'm tempted to point out that if he looked anything like he does now, it's no wonder she propositioned him. "I'm sure you were cute."

"I was eager, if nothing else," he says softly. "I was too eager."

"You were a boy who'd never been with a woman before." I tap my finger against his knee. "No one can fault you for that."

"They did then. They still do." There's a small pause. "Noah always will."

The words carry no surprise at all. I bore witness to the veracity of them the other day when I watched Noah tower over Ben, his pointed finger a spear that was channeling every bit of anger that he'd been carrying within his body for more than a decade. The assault of words was violent, direct and laced with a pain that I never knew existed within Noah.

Talking about Noah isn't going to answer any of my questions. "Can you tell me what happened that day?"

His brow peaks slightly as if he wasn't expecting the question. "That day," he repeats. "The day my mother died?"

I nod. I came here looking for a side of the story that made sense. I want to find the good in Ben because I know it's there. I saw it when he cared for me after my fall. I feel it in his touch. I want to hear him confirm it.

"I mentioned before that we were each responsible for taking care of her at different times." His hand runs over the fabric covering his thigh in a lazy circle. "That day I was taking care of her."

"You said your father had taken Noah to a ball game."

"They left shortly before my friend arrived." His head bows slightly. "My father had a rule that we weren't allowed to have anyone over when we were alone with her."

The weight of the responsibility isn't mine to judge. It's hard to imagine laying a person's fate in the hands of a teenage boy. "Why didn't your mother have a nurse or… why …why wasn't someone with medical training taking care of her?" I stumble through the question.

"She wouldn't hear of it." He shakes his head slightly. "At the time I didn't understand it. I was glad to help, don't get me wrong, but it was a lot for all of us to take on. It was the summer right after we graduated from high school and Noah and I were both given eight hour shifts each day to tend to her every need."

There's no spite within his tone. I can hear the faint hum of regret, but I doubt that he wishes the situation itself were different, only the events of that particular day. He's only spoken of his mother with love in his voice. I hear that now again.

"I had to change the oxygen tank that day." His voice grows raspier and deeper. I can sense all the heavy emotion he's feeling. "I needed to do that right after Noah and my father left."

The oxygen tank was at the core of Noah's insistence that Ben intentionally took their mother's life. He had thrown out accusations about Ben deliberately disconnecting her oxygen supply so she'd die. "Noah talked about her oxygen," I offer, trying to spur on his admission.

"I made a mistake." His voice cracks. "I was in a rush to get to the guesthouse to…" his voice fades with the lost words.

"To spend time with your friend," I offer to keep him moving forward. I don't want pointed details about what took place there. I want to know what happened in the main house when he left his mother.

"Yes." He reaches out to run his fingers over my hand. The touch is intimate, comforting and welcome. "She was in my mother's room with me when I changed the empty tank."

The statement is the first step towards my understanding. He was distracted. He was a virginal teenager in a room with a woman who wanted his body. "You were in a rush to change it?"

"I was." He squeezes my hand within his, his eyes dipping to his lap. "I wanted to get to the guest house. I wasn't thinking clearly."

"What happened?"

Time seems to freeze as he stares at our hands, intermingled together. "I didn't check the hose when I reconnected the new tank. I just assumed that it was fine but it wasn't fastened properly. It fell out of place and she wasn't getting any oxygen."

It's not a slight oversight by any means. It's a life and death mistake that cost him and his brother dearly. "You forgot to check it?" If the words hold any judgment in them, it's not there in my tone.

He looks up from his lap and into my eyes. "My friend kissed me as I set the new tank in place. I'd kissed girls before but this was different. There was a need there. It was overwhelming."

I see the pain in his expression. "What then?"

"I can't remember exactly." He straightens his legs, his back stiffening against the couch. "We kissed more. She told me she wanted to do things to me."

He was caught in his own desire. He let a woman into a space that was forbidden. "You forgot about the tank?"

"I forgot everything." He hesitates a moment, then exhales audibly. "I took her to the guesthouse and she blew me. We spent hours in the bed there, doing everything I wanted. When it was over I fell asleep. The next thing I remember was waking up to the smell of weed, she was gone and my father was crying telling me mother was dead."

Chapter 4

"It was a mistake," I say the words to comfort him but their meaning is lost. A mistake is when you forget to pick up a loaf of bread at the grocery store or the due date on the electricity bill passes before you have a chance to pay it. Those are the mistakes we live with, and deal with. Neglecting to check the connections on your mother's oxygen tank isn't a mistake. I don't want to trivialize this. He lost one of the most important people in his life because he neglected to supply her with the one thing she desperately needed.

His hand brushes over his forehead, stopping to rest against his eyes. "It was stupid. Every decision I made that day was idiotic and selfish."

He has beaten himself up over this for more than a decade. It's a part of him now and although the actual day that it happened may be buried in the past, the emotional toll of it is right there, at the edge of who he is. I saw it when he dropped to his knees beneath Noah's accusations. "You were young."

"It's not an excuse." He jerks his hand from mine. "I was responsible for her care. I broke the rules."

Breaking rules is one thing. Being charged with murder is completely different. It's hard to understand how that happened if it was completely an accident. "Why were you charged with murder?"

He recoils physically at the mention of the word. "I was in a daze. The police came to the house with the ambulance."

That's expected. It's protocol. The same thing had happened the evening my neighbor died when I was a child. The loud blare of the ambulance and police cars had charged me awake. I remember standing on the front porch, staring across the street as they wheeled her lifeless body from her home, her husband shaking with sobs following the stretcher.

"You explained what happened, right?" It's logical. It's an open and shut case in my non-legal brain.

His leg shakes slightly and he grabs hold of his thigh to steady it. "I told them I killed her. I told anyone who would listen to me."

I place my hand against my knee. Its instinct is to jump to his to help calm him. I want to reassure him that I understand because up to this point I do. "You felt responsible for her death."

"I was responsible." The words dart out falling into one another in their haste. "I didn't check the hose on the tank. I walked away."

"There's no way you could have known that she'd die, Ben."

"Kayla." He edges slightly to the left, creating a divide between us. "Alarms were sounding, she was struggling and I wasn't there."

I stare at his face. The guilt is woven into who he is, just as the need to heal is there alongside it. "You didn't do it on purpose."

Abruptly, he faces me, his eyes skimming a path from my forehead to my chin. "You believe in me. It's been so long since anyone has."

The words aren't expected and I'm sure my expression can't mask the surprise. I do believe him. I won't boast and say I'm an incredible judge of character because Parker is proof that I'm not, but with Ben it's different. He's a doctor. His life's mission is to help people get well. He's torn up inside over his mother's death. His reaction to Noah's incessant verbal berating wasn't staged. He was broken, he was remorseful and I saw it with my own two eyes. Just as I'm now seeing a man attempting to forgive himself for what happened when he was barely old enough to drive. "I do believe in you, Ben."

He turns towards me, bending his leg on the couch. "Before my mother died, there was a lot of talk about money."

"Money?" I don't toss the question at him to catch an answer. I know where this is headed. Alexa had unwittingly told me about the inheritance the twins received from their mother's estate when they turned twenty-five.

He leans towards me, his arm reaching across the back of the couch. "My mother changed her will shortly before she died. She included Noah and me in it."

We've shared our bodies in every way the last few weeks. I've held onto him when I've crashed into the most intense orgasms of my life, yet, now as he talks about money and his mother's death it feels more intimate than anything that's taken place in his bed.

"She talked to us about it." His eyes dart down and out of my view. "She didn't go into details about amounts or terms but we understood it was substantial. My mother's family was very wealthy."

I'm listening intently because I know it's going to take me to a place I need to be. He's going to explain why he was arrested for mistakenly forgetting to attach the hose on her oxygen tank. "Was that part of the reason why you were charged with her murder?"

His hands leap to his face. I watch as his body rocks forward slightly. "That's exactly why."

I don't know how to offer comfort so I rest my hand on his calf. "They thought it was a motive?"

"They did," he whispers softly. "I was a teenager, mowing lawns for gas money for my car. When my mother sat us down and explained that we'd each inherit a small fortune if she died, we both said things we shouldn't have."

"Things about money?"

His tongue flits over his bottom lip. "I told Noah that I wished she would die so I could get my own place. It was during an argument with my dad. I regretted it as soon as I said it."

"He told someone about that after she was gone?" I press on wanting to understand the entire scope of what happened in that house between Ben and his brother.

"He was interviewed by the police." His shoulders tense. "He told them I said those things. I told them I killed her and my father told them nothing."

"So they arrested you?" The surprise in my tone isn't as intentional as it sounds. It had to have been an incredibly emotional situation. A line of blame is easy to cast when someone dies. In this case, the hook fell into Ben's lap and he was the one caught up in the firestorm.

"That night." He rubs his wrists. "They handcuffed me and took me to jail."

"I'm sorry." I lean forward to embrace him. I'm doing it as much for him as for myself. "I'm so sorry, Ben."

He pulls me into his chest, adjusting his body so it's as close to mine as possible. "I was terrified. My father didn't come down to help me. There was no one."

"What?" I pull back to look at his face. "That's horrible."

"My best friend's father was an attorney." He eyes me. "He came down there and cleared everything up. The charges were dropped the next day."

The arrest may have been short lived but the damage was far reaching. It's now twelve years later and the wall of agony behind Ben's eyes is proof that the pain of that day has never subsided.

Chapter 5

"My surprise bridal shower is on Sunday at Axel NY. Did you get pink roses for the table settings?"

It's Friday, which means I have two days to convince myself that going to this bridal shower is a good idea. After leaving Ben's apartment last night, I'd gone straight home to bed. The conversation had been too intense for me to even think about anything beyond it. I had barely slept. I'd wanted to stay and cradle him in my arms but I knew that's not what he needed in that moment. He needed to be alone as much as I did.

"It's not a surprise if you're helping plan it, Lex." I run my hand over her shoulder. "You're not supposed to know anything about it. Sadie's going to be devastated."

It's not an exaggeration. Sadie Lockwood is Alexa's matron-of-honor. This bridal shower is everything right now to her. She's worked tirelessly for weeks making sure each detail is exactly the way she wants it to be. Creating a special celebration in honor of Alexa's impending marriage to Noah is Sadie's way of showing how much she treasures them both.

They've been friends since they were children and have held each other's hands through the most trying and important moments in each other's lives. When Sadie needed a heart transplant, Alexa had camped in the hospital waiting room until the surgery was over. When Alexa struggled to adjust to living in Paris for a semester in college, it was Sadie she turned to.

I showed up during Alexa's junior year in college. I'm second best. It's never been a secret. We all know it. The fact that Alexa has chosen Sadie as her matron-of-honor illustrates the dynamic of our friendship to a tee.

"You can handle Sadie." She grabs my hand. "You can tell her that I don't have a clue. A little white lie isn't going to hurt her."

What about my big multi-colored, lights flashing, horns blaring lie? When I first got to Alexa's apartment an hour ago she asked if I'd spoken to Ben. I hadn't answered and although that's technically not an outright lie, it's not who I want to be in this friendship. I want to be open and I want Alexa to understand why I went back to Ben's place to get his side of the story.

"I don't want to lie to Sadie." I try to sound cool and calm. "If she asks me if you know, I'll tell her."

"She's fragile, Kayla." Her words bite into me. "I don't want you to upset her right now."

Right now translates to always. When Alexa had returned from Paris I was the one she confided in about her torrid love affair with a man who was deeply involved with another woman. I had held her while she cried and helped her shed the regret that she'd wrapped herself tightly in. I wasn't supposed to tell Sadie because she knew the man and it would only upset her. It was only one of a string of moments in Alexa's life that Sadie wasn't granted knowledge of. I'm tired of it.

I pull my hand from hers. "She's stronger than you think she is. It's just a surprise party."

She arches her neck back, finally pulling her gaze free from the invitations sitting on the table in front of her. "I know she's strong."

I nod my head as I scroll my finger over the seating chart. "There are a lot of people coming to this wedding. Who knew you and Noah were so popular?"

She tilts her head back, jutting her tongue out at me. "You're not funny. It's so much to organize."

"I'll help in any way that I can," I offer genuinely. I've seen the stress that she's been under the past few weeks. I haven't stepped in to help because my focus has been divided between work and Ben. My new job being Vivian's assistant doesn't stop at five o'clock. She has me emailing, researching and doing odd jobs for her at random times. I feel like a well-paid puppet on a string but it affords me the chance to have my own apartment, so I'm not going to complain.

"Sadie's been great with taking care of most everything."

"I'll text her later to see if she needs help with anything." I don't even blink as I say the words. I mean them.

She spins around in the chair she's sitting in to look up at me. "You know I love you."

The words touch me deeply. I needed to hear them. There's been an undercurrent of misunderstanding floating between us since she learned about Ben and I. "I love you too, Lex."

"I didn't choose her because she's more important to me."

I smile at the proclamation. We haven't openly discussed it. I'd waited for weeks for her to ask me to be her maid-of-honor. A group text message one morning asking me to be a bridesmaid pushed me back into the place I belonged in her life. I was one of four bridesmaids. We're all sorority sisters, all wearing the same color dress, all standing next to Sadie. "I know, Lex."

She pats her hand lightly on her chest. "I had to follow my heart."

"Your heart?" My hand leaps to my own chest. "What do you mean?"

"I talked to Noah about who to choose." She turns both her hands over so the palms are facing up. "Part of me wanted Sadie because we've been friends for so long. The other part of me wanted you because we're so close now."

"What did Noah say?" I cock a brow waiting for her response.

"He told me to listen to my heart." She leans back so her eyes meet mine. "We all need to listen to our hearts more."

"I'm trying to," I say, knowing that for me the words hold more meaning than Lex can ever know.

"You have to, Kayla." She pulls my hands into hers. "I chose Sadie because my heart knew it was right. That's why I chose Noah too. My heart knew he was the man I was meant to be with."

My heart knows what's right for me too. I just have to find a way to convince the people I love that my heart knows best.

Chapter 6

I am in his arms the moment he opens the door of his apartment. It doesn't matter that we haven't spoken at all since the other night. The fact that I didn't call before I got in a cab and came here isn't important to either of us. What does matter is the way his hands reached out to me when he saw me. All that I care about is the touch of his lips against mine and the hunger within his eyes.

"I've been waiting for you," he growls the words into my mouth. "I've been thinking about you every second since you left me."

It's the same for me. My appearance at his door is proof of that. "I've thought about you too," I offer weakly.

His lush lips feather a path over my cheek before they forge hot over mine. I part my mouth to take him in, drowning in the taste of his breath and the softness of his touch. I can't resist him. I don't want to. I only want to feel and let my heart guide me back to being close to him. I need that. I need to be as deeply connected to him, as I was the first night we spent together.

"I want you in my bed." His hands are on me, shedding my body of the sweater I'd pulled on over my dress. "I want to taste you. I need to be inside of you."

I push against him, inching him backwards towards his bedroom. "Ben." His name is heavy as it spreads from my lips onto his. "I want this."

He scoops me up and into his arms in one graceful movement. I hold tight to his shirt as he walks down the hallway and into his bedroom. We don't share words as he tenderly removes my clothing, taking time to kiss a path over my skin as its revealed. I close my eyes, soaking in the touch. This is what I need. This is where I belong.

"Your cunt is so sweet." He's on his knees at the foot of the bed, his head between my legs. "I crave the taste of you, Kayla. I touch myself thinking about how good it is."

I pull my fingers through his thick brown hair, raking my nails across his scalp. "Make me come, Ben."

He pulls his tongue slowly over my smooth slit, stopping to

rest it against my swollen clit. "You're going to come on my face." It's little more than a breathless whisper against my thigh.

I arch my back into the bed, pushing my hips up and into him. He scoops my ass into his palms, pulling me closer. His tongue laps at me with one delicious stroke after another. I cling to his head, losing myself in the pleasure. "It's so good," I moan. "Just like that. I want to come."

His teeth scrape over my clit, coaxing every sensation to the surface. He grunts into my flesh, the whispers of his breath sending me right over the edge.

I cry out his name at full force as the orgasm grips me. I cling to his hair, pulling tightly as I try to dislodge his mouth from me. I'm so aware of every cell that is crying out from the climax. My body is so close to the edge again already. It feels like too much. I can't handle the intensity and I whimper beneath him.

He flips me over with one skillful movement. I'm on my knees. His face between my legs again, kneading the flesh of my buttocks as he circles my entrance with his tongue. He slides two fingers in before he hones in on the spot that throws me back into the rush. I scream his name this time, unable to quiet anything I'm feeling. It's more than I knew existed. My body can't stop its natural reaction to his touch and his desire.

I fall forward lazily on the bed when his hands leave me. I hear the pad of his feet against the hardwood and the unmistakable slam of a drawer. The soft sound of the condom package ripping spurs on my desire even more. The bed shifts when he gets back on.

"I'm ready to fuck you, Kayla." The words are terse, direct and decisive. "That beautiful cunt of yours is going to take all of me."

I whine knowing that it's going to sting. There's a potent bite of pain when he enters me fully. He's wider and longer than any man I've been with. It's only going to be more intense when I'm like this. I'm wet, spread, ready and open to take him.

His hand runs over my ass cheek, stopping to linger on my pussy. "You're so fucking wet. You love when I eat you, don't you?"

It's not a question I can answer. I can't breathe right now. I know what's coming. I know that within seconds he's going to be buried deep within my body, his balls crashing against me as he pumps his cock into me. I whimper from sheer want.

"I can't stand it." The words accompany his entrance. There's no warning at all. He plunges into my body fully and harshly.

I fall forward but his hands grab my waist, pulling me back onto him. He pumps harder, increasing the intensity with each thrust. The only sounds in the still air are his muted grunts, my moans and the slap of his flesh as it hits mine.

"I could fuck you forever." He bites the words out in a deep voice. "I could fuck this body for the rest of my life."

"Do it," I whisper into the pillow. "Do it."

My body lunges forward as his hips grind into mine, each thrust deeper and harder than the last. My name falls from his lips over and over again as he nears his release.

I hold tight to the bed, push my wetness back into him and scream as we both come long and hard.

Chapter 7

"You haven't told them yet, have you?" He's leaning on one elbow when I open my eyes.

I glance past him towards the nightstand. There isn't a clock. "What time is it? I think I fell asleep."

"You're not in a rush to be anywhere, are you?" His lips glide over mine. "I want you to stay the night."

I want that too. It's not an offer he's made before but I grab hold tightly to it. "I'll stay," I try to even my tone. I don't want him to see how eager I am to have this. I can't let him into that part of me yet. It's the part that falls too hard and too fast at the promise of something that my heart has always longed for.

"Good." He scoops me into his arms, pulling my head against his strong chest. "Are you going to tell them?"

This would be so much easier if Noah and Alexa weren't woven so tightly into the fabric of my relationship with Ben. I have to tell them. I can't hide my connection with him forever. Sooner, rather than later, I'm going to have to confess to them both that I'm still sleeping with him.

"I need to tell them." The words aren't minced. There's no doubt there. "I want to tell them soon."

"Noah is never going to change his view of me." He runs his hand lazily over my bare shoulder. "It's been years since it all happened and he's never forgiven me. I wish that he would. I miss him a lot."

I turn to face him directly, soaking in the sight of his beautiful face. "I care about Noah," I begin wanting the words to come out with every intention that is behind them. "I do care about him but I don't live my life for him or for Alexa."

It's true. They are my family in many ways. They helped me when I first came back to New York but they are starting a life together and I need to find my own way too. I can't discount what my heart is feeling simply because it's something that Noah doesn't agree with. I can't change what happened between him and Ben in the past but I can plan for my future. I need to be selfish as I do this.

I have to look out for myself and do what my own heart is telling me is best.

"Did you know Noah before you left New York?" His lips rest against my forehead.

"I did." I lean back wanting to hold his eyes with mine. "I met him a few months before I moved back to Boston."

"Why did you leave here to go back there?"

I knew it was coming. It was inevitable. I can't avoid the subject of my ex-boyfriend indefinitely. I promised myself, after Ben had told me everything about his mother's death, that I wouldn't hold any secrets from him. I want to start our relationship in the most open and honest way that I can. "I went back for a man."

His expression doesn't shift. The only indication that he's heard me at all is in the slight movement of his brow. "A man? What man?"

Names don't matter at moments like this. They don't add any detail to a story that needs to be fleeting and fast. "A man I was in love with."

"This man lives in Boston?"

Good question. "I'm not sure where he is."

"You loved a man and now you don't know where he is?" There's a suggestion of something beyond curiosity in his tone. I can't place it though. "What happened?"

I scratch my chin, needing the brief reprieve to pull all of my thoughts into one place in my mind. "I fell in love with him in high school and…"

"High school?" A smile tears across his lips. "You fell in love with him that long ago?"

"I did," I offer in a small voice. "He was my first love."

His head tilts slightly to the side. "You went back to Boston to be with your first love?"

It sounds romantic coming from his mouth. The words are innocent and sweet and speak of a love that is pure and never ending. That's what I thought I wanted with Parker. The loss of that love was what I was mourning when I boarded the plane for New York. I tried to chase away the pain of Parker's rejection by getting in bed with Ben that first night. I could never have anticipated how Parker's decision to dump me would alter the entire course of my life.

"Kayla?" He scoops my chin into his hand. "Is it too much to talk about this?"

Even if it was, I'd never admit it. I'm next to a man who poured out his heart two nights ago. I listened to him confess to making a mistake that cost him his mother. How can I compare that to losing someone I was never supposed to be with in the first place? "No, it's fine."

"You're sure?" He leans closer, grazing his full lips over mine.

"There's really not much to talk about," I say against his cheek before pulling back to look at him. "We've been on and off for years. I finally moved out here and he decided that he couldn't live without me so I moved back to Boston to be with him."

"You just dropped your entire life here to go back there?"

I hear the surprise in his voice. It's not unexpected. It's the way Alexa and Vivian had reacted to. My own family hadn't hidden the shock when I surprised them with the announcement that I was back with Parker's arm wrapped around me. "I wanted to be with him."

"What changed?" He shifts his entire body so he's leaning on one elbow. "Why did you move back here?"

"It ended," I offer sullenly. Details about who dumped who are trivial now. It seemed so important weeks ago when Ben sat down next to my on the flight. At that moment in time, when my heart was breaking open because Parker had left, I just wanted to forget everything. Now, at this moment, when I'm staring into the eyes of this incredible man, I just want to forget Parker ever existed.

"So, what you're saying…" his voice trails as he wraps his strong arms around. "What you are telling me, Kayla, is that I am your rebound?"

I throw my head back with careless laughter. "You're not my rebound."

"You fucked me that night to forget him."

I stare into his eyes, seeing a glint there that I haven't noticed before. "I fucked you that night because you were hot."

His brows perk. "You think I'm hot?"

I pull in a deep breath, lean forward, press my lips into his and say softly, "I think you're everything."

Chapter 8

Secrets have a way of pulling you apart from within. They fester until they have no place to go but out into the open. It hurt Noah when he saw me leaving Ben's apartment weeks ago. I don't want a repeat of that and I don't want to hide my relationship with his brother any longer.

"Alexa is going to love this bracelet, Kayla." Noah holds the small gift bag in his hand. He'd texted me yesterday asking me to go with him to choose a wedding gift for her. I'd brought him to Whispers of Grace, a boutique jewelry store in Chelsea owned by a friend of Sadie's named Ivy Marlow. I knew we'd find something unique for her here.

"Do you want to grab lunch?" He gestures towards a busy bistro on the corner. "I have no where I need to be today."

"Lex's bridal shower is this afternoon." I glance at my smartphone. "I have time though."

"It's supposed to be a surprise, right?" He walks slowly along the busy sidewalk, his large tattooed frame grabbing glances from almost everyone we pass.

I laugh at the suggestion. "You know that hiding anything from Lex is almost impossible."

He chuckles in return. "She heard Sadie talking to me about it when she was visiting a few weeks ago."

I'm not surprised. Sadie travels to New York City at least a few times a month. Her husband, Hunter, owns Axel NY and she's often there helping him. Her friendship with Alexa is another draw that splits her time between here and Boston.

We settle next to a table in the corner. Even though Noah has become much more comfortable being in public with his facial scar on full display, he still looks for barriers to separate himself from the world. He takes a seat across from me, his back to the restaurant.

"How are things with you?" He nods his head in my direction over the large menu he's holding up. "Work okay?"

I doubt that Noah has any clear idea of what I do for a living. We've never actually discussed it. He knows that I'm considering going back to school to pursue my Master's degree. Beyond that, his grasp on how I spend my days is limited to the few references Alexa makes to it in passing.

"It's fine," I offer back. I didn't come here to talk about the latest project that Vivian has me working on. "It's not exciting."

"Mine is." A broad smile spreads over his lips. "Taking pictures of kids is a hoot."

I admire the forward strides Noah has taken since he got together with Alexa. When he first popped into her life he was a photographer with a singular focus and that was nude women. Alexa had fallen under his spell immediately, spending weeks in his apartment in Boston having her pictures taken. Their unbreakable bond was cemented then and they've never looked back since.

"It sounds like a fun job." I motion towards the approaching waiter.

We order our meals quickly. I'm mindful of the time knowing that within a few hours I need to be at Axel surprising Alexa at the bridal shower she had a heavy hand in planning. I have to somehow convince Sadie that Alexa is oblivious to it all. I definitely have my work cut out for me.

"Kayla?" Noah's hand taps my elbow. "Did you hear me?"

In my wayward daydreams about the shower I don't want to go to, I had blocked everything else out. "No, Noah." I turn in my chair to face him directly. "I'm sorry. What did you say?"

His eyes scan mine as if he's looking for something hidden within. Maybe he is. Maybe he knows full well that there are secrets that I need to share.

"I was asking about Ben." He leans back in the wooden chair that looks as though it's about to burst beneath his weight. "We haven't talked about how you felt when you found out he killed my mother."

I lean back too, pull in a deep breath and stare into his eyes. "He didn't kill her, Noah. We need to talk about that."

***

"Noah," I call to him. He's gaining distance and I need to stop him. "Noah."

He darts his head back and catches a glimpse of me through the crowds on the sidewalk. "Leave me alone."

I push forward, trying to run in my heels. The last thing I want right now is to fall forward and end up back in the ER. "Noah, this is important." I almost scream the words. I can't let him go. I want to clear the air now before this tears Lex and I apart forever. I need her friendship. It is a part of what grounds me and Noah grounds her, so I'm going to do whatever it takes to end this now.

He stops and turns abruptly, causing those around him to stop dead in their tracks for fear of running into him. "I don't want to discuss this with you."

"You ran off in the restaurant." I push the words out through heavy breaths. "Please talk to me."

He holds out his arm in a comforting gesture. I lean against it to catch my breath. "I won't discuss Ben with you, Kayla."

"Do you even know the full story of what happened that day?" My tone is more accusatory than I mean for it to be. I don't want to get into an argument with him. If I'm being completely honest, my desire to talk to him is for purely selfish reasons. I just want him to accept that I'm seeing Ben. I need that for me and although I know it's unrealistic, those parts of me that want the perfect life aren't willing to let it go without a fight.

He pulls me to the left. "Sit," he orders as he points to a wooden bench that is sitting near the entrance of a hotel. "Just sit."

I do as I'm told, not so much to give in to Noah, but to rest my weary feet. I'd chased him for more than two blocks after he'd stormed out of the bistro. "Thank you."

He crouches in front of me, resting his hands on either side of me. "I told you to stay away from him. You went back to see him, didn't you?"

Noah's emotions are all right there at the surface. There's no masking the anger and frustration. He's pissed at me. "I did."

"Why the fuck would you do that?"

His hand balls into a fist next to me. I'm not fearful that he'll hurt me. He won't. I trust Noah with my life. I know that he's in pain. I know that my relationship with Ben is a constant, and unwelcome, reminder of the day he lost his mother.

"I care about him."

He leans closer, his breath hot on my forehead. "How can you care about a man who has hurt so many people?"

"Noah." I clench my hands together in my lap. My intention isn't to hurt him. I'm doing that already and it's breaking me a little inside. I know about his past. I know that he was stabbed and the physical and emotional scars of that pushed him into being a recluse for years. I know he lives with a depth of internal pain that I can't comprehend. I've heard enough from Lex to understand. "He's not who you think he is."

"Really?" He cocks a brow and stares straight through me. "He killed her, Kayla. Do you need evidence of that before you'll believe it?"

"You don't have any evidence of that, Noah," I push back. "Tell me what evidence you have."

He mutters a curse word under his breath. "He didn't connect her oxygen tank, Kayla. He just didn't do it. There's no way that was just a mistake like he says."

"Why?" I grab the edge of the bench for strength. "Why are you so convinced that he did it on purpose?"

"Both of us," he begins before he waves two large fingers in my face. "Both of us were trained on how to change those tanks. He'd done it dozens of times before. There's no way in hell he just forgot to do it that day."

"People make mistakes, Noah." I look past him to where pedestrians are strolling by, completely oblivious to the gravity of our discussion. "He made a mistake."

"That's bullshit," he hisses the words at me. "He knew what he was doing. He didn't connect it and then he went to the guesthouse to get high while she died."

"He didn't." I pinch the bridge of my nose. "It wasn't so he could get high. He was too excited to be with the woman who came to see him after you and your father went to the ballgame."

"What? What are you talking about?" He points at my mouth. "You don't know what you're saying. There was no woman, Kayla. My father didn't see her when he went to tell Ben about our mother. Ben made that up because he felt so guilty."

"He did not," I whisper the words into the air between us, my belief in them unwavering. "Ben told me about her. Her name was Samantha. He lost his virginity to her that day."

Chapter 9

"Did you text her to tell her you'd be late to the bridal shower." He nods towards my smartphone in my palm.

"I did. I told her I'd be there within the hour. She's having a blast. I doubt that Lex will even miss me." Judging by the excitement in her voice, I know that she won't notice if I don't show up at all.

He motions towards a chair next to the dining room table. "Sit, Kayla."

His commands are wearing on me. After I'd brought up the woman Ben was with when their mother died, Noah's face had gone ashen. He'd pulled me to my feet, hailed a cab and ordered me into it. Now, we're sitting face-to-face in his apartment.

"How do you know about the woman? About Sammy?"

Sammy? That wasn't what Ben called her. "You mean Samantha?"

"Kayla." His hand taps my fingers as he ignores my question. "Tell me what Ben said about Sammy."

I wish I could speak to Ben. We haven't discussed this. The possibility of my having a pointed discussion with Noah about his brother's first sexual partner seemed incomprehensible until a few minutes ago. Now, I'm in the middle of it and I need to own what I've already put out there. "He didn't say much, Noah. Just that she was his first and it happened that day."

He's on his feet. "He actually told you he lost his virginity that day?"

I nod. This is too personal of a conversation for me to be having with Ben's brother. I don't share the details of my first experience with even my closest friends. I'd be mortified if anyone was passing those details around. I need to talk to Ben. "I think I should talk to Ben about this."

He rubs his index fingers against his temples. "Kayla. This is very important. I need you to think hard about what Ben told you."

"How does any of this matter, Noah?" I'm exasperated. I wanted to talk to him about forgiveness and second chances. I wanted him to understand that Ben made a horrific mistake and emotionally he's paying for it every single day. I don't want to continue to discuss the woman Ben was intimate with while his mother was dying.

"It matters more than you know." He wrings his hands together. "Kayla, please."

I stare at his face. The color hasn't returned. His eyes are darting from me to the wall behind my head. I pull on the edge of my skirt. I feel exposed and vulnerable. I feel as though I'm giving away my own secrets, even though they belong to Ben.

"Noah." I hear the plea in my own voice. "I don't know if I should be sharing this."

He moves swiftly, his hand pressing against the table next to me as his breath races over my forehead. "I need you to tell me right now word-for-word what my brother said to you."

I look into his eyes. I see desperation. He may be trying to mask it, but he's frantic for answers that only I can provide right now. I swallow hard. "He told me that she came over right after you and Ron left."

"Sammy came to the house that day?" He leans back slightly. "You're sure he said it was that day?"

"I'm positive." My voice is strained. "He said that she came into the room where your mother was."

His mouth thins. "Go on."

"She kissed him." I pull my hands to my lips. "He said it wasn't like any other kiss before."

"Sammy kissed him?"

"She told him that she was going to do things to him." My voice cracks at the admission. "They were sexual things."

"How could he have been a virgin then?" The question isn't directed at me judging by the way he's speaking softly in the direction of the floor. "He was too old to still be a virgin. I'd slept with so many…"

I jump in out of necessity. I don't want to hear about his sexual conquests when he was a teenager. I need him to help ground me. I feel lost within our conversation. "Noah, he was a virgin until that day."

Without warning his hand slams the table next to me, causing the vase of fresh flowers to teeter precariously. He reaches to balance it, his arm sweeping past my face. "I can't believe this."

I grab hold of his forearm. "Please, Noah. I don't understand."

His eyes float over mine but they're distant and detached. "Kayla, what else? Tell me what else he said."

I hesitate only briefly before I answer, "Ben said that he removed the empty oxygen tank and put the new one in place but that he was in a rush and didn't check to make sure the hose was connected properly. He said it fell away at some point and your mother died then."

"Christ." The word falls slowly from his lips. "What else?"

I can't delve into the details of what Ben shared about their intimacy because there weren't any beyond her taking him in her mouth. "He said he woke up when your father showed up and smelled marijuana. He said she was gone by then."

"Fuck." His hands race to his face as he stumbles backwards into the chair. "Fuck, no."

"Noah." I reach to grab hold of his hand to steady him but he recoils sharply. His entire body pushes back away from me. "Noah, tell me what's going on."

"Leave." His hand floats into the air between us. "Just go."

I sit in silence for not more than a minute before I pick up my purse and pull myself to my feet. "Do you want me to call Lex? Should I tell her about this?"

His head shakes violently from side-to-side. "Not a word. Don't say anything to her or Ben."

I don't respond. I turn on my heel and walk quietly towards the door while listening to the dull thud of his fist hitting the table again and again.

Chapter 10

"This is the best bridal shower ever." Alexa pulls on my hair causing my head to fly back.

"Shit." I reach to grab my neck. "What the hell, Lex?"

"You're in a horrible mood," she slurs the words into my face. "Have a drink, or two or ten."

She's drunk. She was drunk the moment I arrived and it's only gotten worse in the hour that I've been here. I can't blame her though. This is her celebration. She's carefree and excited about jumping into married life. I, on the other hand, am trying to decipher exactly what happened between Noah and me earlier.

"You were so late." She pats me on the top of the head. "I should send you to the principal's office."

"Teacher jokes?" I smile. "You're actually telling teacher jokes?"

"What can I say?" She shrugs her shoulders causing the drink in her hand to tip to the left.

I reach for it and her, steadying her back on her feet. "You should have some coffee."

"I have the day off tomorrow." She raises the glass high above her head. "I don't have to think about anything for two whole days."

I'm envious. It's not because she's marrying her life partner and their path together is right there at her feet. I'm jealous that she's so blissfully unaware of what happened earlier. I wish I was oblivious to it as well. "You're lucky," I say it with genuine sincerity.

"You'll find a guy too one day, Kayla." Her hand drifts to my chin. "You're so pretty. You're going to find a man just like Noah who will love you so much."

The irony in her words isn't lost on me. I have found a man who resembles Noah physically but is diametrically different from him in almost every other way. "I know that I will, Lex."

"Maybe you can track Parker down." Her eyes light up. "He loved you once."

I know the intention behind her words isn't to spear through me the way they do. "I don't want to talk about Parker."

"You must miss him." She brings her drink to her lips, emptying it in one large swallow. "That's why you hooked up with Noah's brother, right?"

"I guess it was," I whisper. I don't think about it anymore. It's hard to pull myself back to that airplane and the moment when Ben sat down and we started talking. It was impossible not to notice how attractive he was at first glance. The soft touch of his hand as it brushed against mine when he handed me the glass of water the flight attendant first gave to him, had sent an electric current through me. When he leaned over to comment on how cute the voice of the child sitting behind us was, I'd smelled his cologne. I wanted him then for who he was, not just for the escape his body offered me. I had to move on from Parker's rejection and Ben was the first step.

"You wouldn't have done it if you knew he who he was, right?"

The question is ripe with expectation. I can't answer it. I wouldn't have cared if he would have given me his entire name that night and I would have connected the dots on the spot. My connection to Ben had nothing to do with Noah. It didn't then and it doesn't now. "I don't know."

"What does that mean?" She plops her ass in the chair next to me. "You would have fucked him even knowing he was Noah's asshole brother?"

The force of the words isn't necessary. She's not speaking from her experiences with Ben. Everything that is coming out of her mouth is a reflection of what she's heard Noah saying. "Don't call him an asshole."

She tosses her head back in wild laughter. Many of the guests at the shower turn to look at us, smiles radiating across their faces. They think we're having fun. They believe I've said something that has pushed Alexa into a place of pure joy. Not one of them can know what's floating between us. "You need to stop defending him, Kayla."

"You need to stop accusing him of things you know nothing about." I bite my lip to try and curb my growing anger. "You only know what Noah has told you."

"What more is there to know?" She slams the glass in her hand down so violently I'm shocked that it doesn't shatter.

This isn't the time. It's sure as hell not the place. I need to stop this now before it becomes the only memory she has of this night. "Nothing, Lex. There's nothing more to know."

She cocks a perfectly sculpted blonde brow. "You're lucky you got away from him before he hurt you too."

I fidget in my seat. My overwhelming need to defend Ben is right there at the surface. "Have fun at your party, Lex."

"I will." She calls over her shoulder before she pulls two women I don't know into a tight embrace.

Chapter 11

"Kayla, no. Please no." His hands caress my cheeks. "I'm going to blow my load."

I want that. I've wanted it for days. I need to be close to him, just like this. It's helping rid my mind of the conversation I had with Noah three days ago.

"Fuck," he hisses the word out above me.

I lick harder. My tongue is tracing a ring around the head of his thick cock. My hands are gripping it, slowly stroking it. "You taste so good," I purr as I pull him out of my mouth.

"I need this so much." His hands move to my hair. "You suck me so good."

I do. He doesn't need to tell me. I can feel it myself in the way his cock jumps when I lick the length of it. I hear it in his groans when my hands cup his heavy balls and squeeze. "I want you to come in my mouth."

He moans loudly. His hips rock into me as his cock swells even more. It's large. I've struggled every time I've taken it into my mouth but my desire to please him overwhelms everything else. I bob my head up and down finding a slow, easy rhythm that draws a low grunt from deep within his body.

"You're so good, Kayla."

I take the approval and run with it. I lean forward sliding more of his glorious cock into my mouth. I'm rewarded with a burst of hot pre cum that slides effortlessly down my throat. I fist him harder, jerking the root in my hand as my lips slide over the head again, and again.

"I'm going to fuck your beautiful mouth."

I whimper at the promise. I brace one hand against the bed, using it to steady myself for the onslaught of thrusts he's about to gift me with. He doesn't disappoint as his large hands weave deeper into my hair, pulling it at its roots, the momentary burst of pain pooling the desire between my legs.

I'm still dressed. He's completely nude with his head thrown back. "I'm so close."

I want it. I've craved this since he ordered me onto my knees in the shower at the shitty motel. I loved that he took control of me then. I want it still. Knowing that he is taking all of this pleasure from me is making my own body ache for release.

I know the instant he's about to come before his lips betray his need.   "Goddammit," he spits it into the air just as the first stream shoots into my mouth. I moan from the taste and from the sounds falling off his beautiful lips. I look up, completely captivated by the sight of him in total ecstasy.

I pull back slightly allowing his desire to flow onto my lips. I lick it all, kissing the tip of his now semi-erect cock as he leans back into the bed.

The silence is thick, the only sound between the two of us the deep groans I'm making, as I taste everything this man has given to me.

***

"I have to catch my breath before I fuck you."

I smile at his desire to please me. I wanted to come so badly when I was on my knees on the floor but now, moments later, as I'm nude and wrapped in his arms, nothing matters but this closeness. I don't need the orgasm. I'm not chasing the climax, I just want to stay in this space with him and never let go.

"Did you fall asleep?" His lips graze my hair as I rest my cheek against his smooth cheek. "You fell asleep, didn't you?"

I race my finger around his nipple. "I'm wide awake. I was just thinking."

"About what?"

Noah. Alexa. Samantha. Life.

"Nothing in particular." I opt for the least complicated of all answers. The internal debate that has been pulling at every corner of me since I left Noah's place hasn't quieted itself down at all. I want to tell Ben that I shared intimate details of our conversation with Noah. I need to tell him that. I know I silently promised Noah I wouldn't but he's not the man I'm resting against now. He's not the man I think about virtually the entire day. Ben is and he deserves to know my secrets, just as he's shared his with me.

"Is it about him?" His voice is low and prodding. The question doesn't contain any ambiguity at all. He's asking about Noah.

"Him?" I throw it back at him so I can give myself a moment to think about where to start. Do I explain that Noah brought him up first and in my haste to defend him, I said things about the day their mother died that I shouldn't have? Or is it best to let him lead the conversation so I can gauge how much he's ready to hear? My initial inclination to confess all when I got here was halted when he answered the door completely nude.

"The guy," he begins before swallowing hard. "Your boyfriend."

My boyfriend? Parker? I'm in Ben's arms, after taking him down my throat and giving him a mind numbing orgasm and he's asking me about Parker? "Are you talking about the man who left me?"

"Yeah." His hand strokes my hair. "That guy."

It's real. He's actually bringing up the man who broke my heart while I'm naked next to him. "Why would we talk about him again?"

He pulls on my arms, coaxing me to look at him. I acquiesce, resting my elbows on his chest. "You seem distant tonight. I guess I just thought it was about him."

"Why would you think that?" I try not to sound as defensive as I feel. The last person I want to discuss with Ben is Parker. "I don't think about him."

"You have to think of him." He pushes a stray hair off my forehead. "We all think about the people we loved every now and again."

"Do you think about the women you love when you're in bed with me?" It may be petulant and biting, but it's a valid question. "Do you do that?"

His hand flies up to ward me off and the gesture only irks me more. "I was just asking why you were quiet."

"I had your cock in my mouth. It's hard to talk when that's going on." I nod my head down the bed.

The corner of his lips dart up. "You did and it was crazy good."

"Don't ask me about him anymore, Ben." I want to stop the Parker talk in its tracks. I haven't thought about him in days. The last time was when Alexa brought him up at her bridal shower. "I don't think about him."

"You're over him?"

"Completely," I say with conviction. "He's my past. I'm looking to the future."

"Me too, Kayla." He wraps his arms around me. "Me too."

Chapter 12

"I'm going to apply for the Master's program soon." I hold a piece of paper in front of me. "I need two references. I know it's not something we've ever talked about but…"

"Give it to me." Noah pulls the paper from my grasp with a heavy swipe. "I'll give you a glowing reference."

"It's just that you're impressive." I realize the moment the words leave my lips that they sound misplaced. "I mean I know that people find your work really impressive."

"You don't?" A smirk accompanies his cocked brow.

"I do."

"Don't lie," he teases, as his eyes stay glued to the paper.

"I appreciate you doing this." I mean it. I had considered asking Ben for no more than a brief second. Our connection was too new to ask him to provide something like this. It wasn't that I thought he'd balk at the idea. It was more that I didn't want to request something that made him uncomfortable. I was feeling enough of that myself after he brought up Parker in his post orgasmic state.

"Alexa got drunk at her bridal shower." A whisper of a smile floats over his mouth. "She was pretty funny when Sadie brought her home."

I can't help but smile too. "I saw her for a few minutes. She was definitely enjoying herself."

His eyes finally drift up from the paper to settle on my face. "She mentioned that you two talked about Ben."

I'm shocked that she remembered at all. I wasn't sure she would but now that I know she brought it up, it's opened a door for me with Noah. "It was brief. I didn't tell her anything."

"You've seen Ben since then, right?" The anger that would have been wrapped around that question days ago isn't there anymore.

"Yes."

"Did you talk to him about what we discussed?" His tone is low and direct.

I shake my head. "I didn't." Why would I? Ben was too busy trying to gather information on my asshole of an ex-boyfriend. Once that conversation ended we both drifted to sleep and in our morning rush to get to work, neither of us discussed anything beyond meeting for dinner later in the week.

"I don't have a lot of friends," he says softly. "I mean I have Alexa. I don't need a bunch of friends, but there's no one I can talk to about this."

I know that the *this* he's referring to is his brother. "What is it?"

He looks up and his eyes search my face momentarily. "It's about Ben and what we were talking about the other day."

I want to help Noah and it's not for purely selfish reasons. Obviously listening to him talk about his brother gives me more insight into the man I'm sharing my body with, but it also is pulling me closer to Noah. I'm seeing a side of him that is strictly reserved for Alexa. I've only heard about it when she's confided in me about their relationship. "What about it?"

"I'm not sure how much Ben has told you about his arrest?"

It's an open-ended question. He wants me to fill in those blanks. "Not a lot," I offer back as a starting point.

"Did he tell you why they arrested him?"

I run my tongue over my top lip as Ben's words about Noah's discussion with the police pours through my memory. "He said there were a lot of things that contributed to that."

He taps his hand against the dining room table. We're sitting in exactly the same places we were when he grilled me about Sammy. "The police questioned me. They questioned our father too."

Even if I didn't know that information because Ben told me, I wouldn't be surprised. It was an investigation surrounding their mother's death. It only made sense that everyone in the home was interviewed. "He told me that, Noah."

He traces his index finger along the edge of the paper I handed to him. "Did he tell you what I said to the police?"

"Only bits and pieces."

"It was mostly about my perception of what happened. " He sighs. "I was pretty torn up about my mother's death."

"You all were," I say carefully. "I'm sure you were all distraught that day."

"I was pissed." His hand fists on the table. "I couldn't believe she was gone."

I'm insightful enough to understand that neither of the twins was prepared for their mother's death. Despite the fact that she'd been struggling with her health for weeks, her death hit them both with the impact of a sledgehammer. It threw their entire family into an emotional tailspin that they've yet to recover from. I don't respond because I can't find the words to describe the sorrow I feel for them both.

"Ben didn't say much after she died. He shut down." He exhales quickly. "The police tried talking to him and he kept saying that he killed her."

The stress of knowing that he hadn't checked her oxygen tank is still a heavy burden that Ben carries with him. I can't imagine what that felt like on the shoulders of a teenage boy. "He felt guilty."

"That night changed all of our lives." His face pales. "Ben lost all his scholarships. He couldn't go to the school he wanted to."

I didn't know that. I had assumed that after he was released, that he'd thrown himself into his studies. "He's never talked about that."

"His life fell apart." His breath hisses out. "It was all so messed up. I couldn't stand the sight of him so he left to go live with my grandparents."

My heart aches at the thought of Ben's life being thrown so off course because of what happened that day. "He's built a good life for himself."

He doesn't acknowledge my statement at all. "He wrote me letters after he moved in with them, but I ripped them up. I never read one. I wanted nothing to do with him."

"He's a good person who made a horrible mistake." I stand up. I need air. I have to get out of here. "He has to live with what he did every single day."

"I do too," he whispers as I turn to walk away. "I do too, Kayla."

Chapter 13

"Are you ever going to tell me what kind of doctor you are?" I push on his knee under the small table with my own.

"I'm a very…"

I dart my hand into the air and push it against his lips. "Don't say you're a very good doctor, Ben. I want a real answer."

He pushes my hand into his lips, giving my palm a most kiss. "It's a real answer."

"I want the scientific answer," I wince when I say the words. "No, that's not what I meant."

He chuckles at my obvious lack of knowledge. "I'm a primary care physician."

I'm not up on the medical lingo that I should be considering I'm sleeping with a doctor. "What exactly does that mean?"

He squeezes my hand in his. "It means I work in the emergency room and I like it there."

"You'll always work there?"

"Not forever." His eyes flit over my shoulder to the entrance of the cafeteria. "For now it's where I want to be."

I don't probe more because he hasn't ever offered details about his work. I'd imagined that his drive to be a doctor was triggered by his mother's illness and the guilt he still carries because of her death, but that might be my overly active imagination pushing those two events together.

"Let's talk about your work."

"Let's not." I push my back into the uncomfortable chair. I've spent the majority of the past week organizing Vivian's file cabinet. It's taxing, boring and makes each day longer than the previous one. I'm looking forward to getting back to school part-time mainly because I need more stimulation for my brain.

"Don't say I never asked about it." He playfully tips his chin across the table at me. "What else has been going on in your life lately? You're still part of Noah's wedding party?"

It's a question that is too shallow considering the depth of the turmoil that surrounds his brother and him. I hate talking about the wedding. We haven't discussed how utterly fucked up it is that I'm going to his twin brother's wedding and he's not. I want to invite him. I want the past to wash under a bridge so that Ben can be there to congratulate his brother as he starts on the path to wedded bliss. It's an impossible situation that I'm stuck in the middle of. "I'm still part of that, yes."

"How does that make you feel?"

Like shit.

That's what I want to say. I feel anxious and nervous about it. I cringe when I know that I have to see Lex now to discuss the music, menu or what the place cards should look like. Every time she hugs me I feel a drive to confess my deepest secrets which all involve her soon-to-be husband and his twin brother. It's no wonder she chose Sadie to be her matron-of-honor. I'm a horrible friend to her but I can't tell Ben that so instead I say, "I want Lex to be happy so I'll do what I can to make the wedding perfect."

Liar, Kayla. You did that way too easily.

"I need to get back to work soon." He glances at his silver wristwatch. "Do you want to meet up tonight?"

It's casual. This entire thing feels as though it's moving towards more casual. I doubt it's my imagination telling me that. I can sense it and feel it. "Are you hooking up with other women?"

His shoulders tense as his eyes scan my face. "Where did that come from?"

A simple *no* would have sufficed just fine, Doctor.

I scratch my finger over my ear. "I'm just curious."

He stretches his legs beneath the table, kicking my foot in the process. "Sorry."

I don't respond because I'm suddenly aware that I've been investing countless hours in trying to mend his broken relationship with his brother. Why am I doing that when we've never discussed being exclusive? He's not offering anything beyond uncomfortable silence now, which I know is, code for '*hell, yes, I'm fucking other women.*'

"I need to get back to work." I'm lying. I have the rest of the day off and my hope was that he'd steal a few minutes away to join me in his bed. "I've got a lot to do today."

His hand bolts to my wrist, pulling it firmly into his grasp. "Kayla, sit."

Apparently commands are part of the twins' mutual DNA. "Why?"

"I want to say this right." His hand slides across my wrist to cup my hand. "I don't want to fuck it up."

I stare at our hands unable to pull my gaze to his handsome face. I don't want this to be the moment when he pulls a Parker on me and tells me it's over. We haven't really started yet and losing him now would rip me to shreds. "Fuck up what, Ben?"

"I know you just ended things with that guy in Boston weeks ago." He swallows hard before pushing a rush of air out between his lips. "I've been trying to figure out where your head is with that."

Seriously? All those random Parker related questions in bed were about this? "I've told you where it's at." I feel a driving need to reiterate the point. "I'm over him."

"Don't date anyone else then." His hand pulls mine towards him. "Don't fuck anyone. Let me be the only one."

Chapter 14

"Ben was born exactly seven minutes after I was." He points to the clock on the wall in the restaurant. "Seven minutes."

"You're older than him?" I don't try and mask the fact that I'm not shocked by the admission. "Somehow that doesn't surprise me at all."

"I'm more mature." He grins. "You think that's it, right?"

"No, Noah." I take a small sip of the herbal tea I ordered. "That's not it. I think it's because you're so bossy."

"I'm bossy?" He runs his finger along the rim of the paper coffee cup. "Did Alexa tell you I'm bossy?"

"Alexa?" I cock a brow. "I don't need anyone to tell me. I see it myself."

"Don't take this the wrong way, Kayla..." His eyes dart around the near empty café before they settle back on my face. "Don't let this get to your head but you're actually kind of fun to hang out with."

"You'll never admit that again, will you?" I push my hand towards him across the table. "If I tell Lex you said that, you're going to deny it."

"I will." He nods slowly. "It's our little secret."

Correction. It's one of our little secrets. The list is growing longer day-by-day. Today, while Alexa is at yoga and Ben is on duty in the ER, Noah and I are meeting in a small café in mid-town. He asked me to meet him here via text message an hour ago. I agreed without thought. Noah is my direct line to Ben's past and his future. I want to understand everything about the man I'm now officially in an exclusive relationship with.

"Has Ben ever talked to you about this?" His hand traces a path down the scar on his cheek. I don't stare at it. I never have. When I first met Noah it was impossible to ignore. It's long, jaded and speaks of the violence of that night.

I answer without any hesitation. "We don't talk about you that much."

"Why not?"

Anyone who doesn't know Noah Foster may find that question arrogant. That's not why he spit it out. He wants to matter to his brother. I've seen it in his eyes and hear it in his voice more and more. "We talk about other things."

"Like what?" he presses.

"Things that are none of your business, Noah." I raise my cup towards him.

It's the first time I've ever seen him blush. He pulls his head down so swiftly that I only get a fleeting glimpse of it but it's tender and gives me witness to the parts of him that Lex is always fawning over. "I was just wondering if he told you anything about the night I was stabbed."

He doesn't look up as the question sits in stillness between us. I know that the stabbing only occurred a few years ago and it's been my understanding that Noah and Ben were estranged at the time. "You weren't talking to each other then, were you?"

"No." His answer is quick and abrupt.

"Why would he ask me about it?" I can't connect the dots at all. "Did he even know you were stabbed?"

His eyes pull up and onto my face. "He knew, Kayla. My father called to tell him and he was on the first flight to Boston to see me."

I don't know how to absorb that other than one twin needing to be by his brother's side after a horrific incident. "I'm not surprised. Ben's a caring person."

"It didn't go well." He hesitates as his eyes travel the length of the restaurant. "I was in a bad place."

"You didn't want to see him?" I'm not sure why I'm asking the question at all. Judging by the one time I've seen Noah and Ben in the same room together, I doubt that Noah has ever been eager to spend any time with his brother since that morning their mother died.

"I tried to kill him."

***

"I can get you another cup." The barista daps at the tea stain on my jeans. "I'll go get it now."

I push her hand away. "No, please. I'm fine." I'm not fine at all. Noah's words had pulled every ounce of strength from me and my hand instantly gave way. The moment the hot tea hit my lap, I'd jumped. He was there, almost immediately, his hand wiping away the liquid.

She mutters something incomprehensible under her breath as she scoops up a handful of damp paper napkins and walks back behind the counter.

"Did you burn yourself?" He's in the chair next to me now, his hand holding tightly to mine. "You're white as a ghost, Kayla."

That has nothing to do with the scorching liquid that splashed all over me and everything to do with the fact that he just told me he tried to kill Ben. "I'm okay," I whisper. "I'm okay."

"I can take you to the…" He halts himself. "Is there a doctor I can take you to see?"

I stare at his face. We're both fully aware of the irony in the question. "My jeans caught most of it. I didn't get burned."

"Good." He holds his gaze on mine. "I'm sorry I didn't know you'd react like that."

I push my hands into my lap. "How did you think I'd react? You just told me that you tried to kill Ben." I motion towards his face. "I heard you say it."

"Something snapped inside of me that morning." He rakes his hand through his short brown hair. "They must have sedated me when they brought me in after the stabbing. I was out of it. I was hallucinating."

I've never been on strong painkillers so I have nothing to go by other than the stories I've heard on the news about what people are capable of when they're under the influence of strong narcotics. "I can't imagine what you were going through."

"Alexa told you I killed the man who stabbed me in self defense, right?"

I nod. I don't want to give an actual voice to that. I know that Alexa felt that she was betraying Noah's trust when she shared those details with me. I don't want this conversation to run off its path. I need to understand what happened between Noah and Ben that morning.

"I didn't expect to see Ben." He scrubs his hand over the back of his neck. "He was actually the last person I thought I'd see when I woke up that day."

"You were asleep before he arrived?"

"I was sedated," his correction is subtle. "When I first opened my eyes I couldn't place where I was. The last thing I remembered was the sting of the knife when it..." his voice trails as his hand leaps to his cheek.

"Then Ben was there?" I want him to tell me what happened. I'm eager to hear it.

He pulls his gaze back to my face. "I saw him. I hadn't seen him since he left to live with my grandparents."

I had assumed at some point that the two of them would have ended up in the same place. I can't mask the surprise I feel knowing their lives became so utterly separate.

"I felt this searing pain in my cheek." His voice cracks slightly at the remembrance. "I asked out loud what had happened to me."

I scratch the edge of my nose. "Ben was the one who answered?"

His head tilts to the left with a slight nod of his chin. "I heard his voice before I saw him."

I close my eyes imagining the scene in Noah's hospital room that morning. The pain of the slashes would have been intense and the emotional burden of the events that led up to the scarring would have been overwhelming. Add to that, the appearance of a brother he hated and it was a perfect storm of rage and revenge.

"I called out his name and he walked to the side of the bed." He swallows so hard that it's audible." I remember turning slowly and seeing him there. His face was perfect. He was staring at me. He told me I'd been stabbed in the face and body."

"God," I whisper under my breath unable to contain everything I'm feeling.

He bows his head low. "I lunged out of the bed and onto him. I pushed him against the wall."

I feel tears racing to the surface. I can't stop them. The vision of Ben being assaulted is pulling my stomach into knots.

"I hit him over and over again," he sobs. "I broke his nose and knocked out a tooth."

I want to ask the obvious question but I can't pull it to my lips. "Did he..." that's all I can get out before I bury my face in my hands.

"He didn't fight back, Kayla." Tears stream down the scar and into his short beard. "He just let me punch him until my father and the doctor finally pulled me off."

Chapter 15

I stare at his handsome face. There's no way I ever would have known that his perfect nose was broken at one time.

"Do you think I'm good looking?" He turns sharply, catching my gaze with his. "You're staring at me."

"I think you may be the best looking man in this room."

He throws his head back in laughter. "I'm the only man in this room."

He is. He came to my place after he'd finished a very long shift. Now we're lying in my bed, after sharing a shower. I'm eager to feel him inside of me but I want to savor this moment for as long as I can. It's quiet, calm and I can tell he's relaxed.

"I need to go to Boston this weekend." His lips rest against my forehead. "I don't like the idea of leaving you here."

"I can come with you." It's an eager offer. I'm growing more and more attached to him as each day passes. I feel closer to him today than I ever have before and I know, logically, that a big part of that is tied into the conversation I had with Noah. I haven't brought it up with Ben because I don't know how to. I need to at some point. I can't keep everything I know about him a secret much longer.

"It's a boring medical conference." His hand moves from my shoulder to my back. "You're busy with wedding plans anyways."

A flash of disappointment races over me. He's right though. The wedding is fast approaching and I haven't been giving Alexa the time or attention she deserves. I need to get my mind back into that place where helping her is my priority. This wedding is her dream come true and I want to make it as special of a day as I can for not only her, but Noah too.

After Noah had told me about what happened after his stabbing, we'd said goodbye with an embrace. He'd held tight to me, burying his face in my hair asking me to wait until he could talk to Alexa about things before I told Ben. It was a repeat of the day he barged into Ben's apartment and started throwing accusations out about his role in their mother's death. I can't help but feel I'm headed towards another cliff like that without any brakes to slow me down. I just want this all to be over. I want Noah and Ben to sit down and work out their differences.

"You're drifting somewhere again." His hand races down my back towards my ass. "I need to do something to get you to pay attention to me."

I lean back wanting to feel his lips on mine. "Kiss me," I whisper as I look into his eyes.

He shifts his body away from mine slightly, freeing his other hand. He brushes my chin, pulling my face to his before his lush lips glide over mine. His kiss is wet, deep and hungry. I open my mouth to let his tongue slide next to mine. My hands run over his smooth chest, stopping to soak in how hard every part of his body is.

He rolls me over with little effort until I'm on my back. His mouth leaves mine, traveling with slow, languid licks to my neck. I whimper from the brush of his lips against my flesh, knowing that he's on a path to my nipples.

I arch my back as he pulls one tight, hard bud into his mouth. His teeth clamp down on it; drawing every sensation my body has to offer to the surface. I feel my legs fall open, my sex is wet and needy and aching to have him inside of me.

"Your cunt is already so wet." His eyes travel down my body. "I love how greedy it is for me."

I moan from the weight of the words. They're full of desire. "Fuck me, Ben."

His hand cups my sex. "You want me to fuck this?"

I groan into the still air, my hips grinding into the mattress, searching for more stimulation. "I need to come."

"You need to come with me inside of you." He moves slowly and deliberately, dragging his large body over mine. "I have to get a condom."

His hand leaves my pussy and I whimper from the lost touch. My hand jumps down to replace it. I pull my fingers through my folds, moaning loudly.

"Christ," he growls as he pulls the condom over his erection sheathing it. "You're making me want to blow my load already. Do you touch yourself like that when you're thinking of me?"

I own it. I need to own it. "I do."

He crawls back onto the bed, stopping to kneel next to me. "Show me more."

I circle my clit with my index finger before I slide it deeply into my slick channel. "I do this when I think about you fucking me."

"I'm the only man you think about when you fuck yourself?"

I nod, my voice lost as he climbs on top of me. I reach to grab hold of him. I'm desperate for his touch.

His hand dips into my sex, pulling his fingers through it. "You're so wet. I'm going to slide my cock into you. I'm going to fuck you so hard."

I pull on his shoulders. "Now."

"Now." The word comes from the deepest part of him as he drives his cock into me in one motion.

I open my eyes, stare into his and let my body take all the pleasure he's giving to me as he fucks me hard and fast until we scream each other's names as the rush of an orgasm washes over both of us.

Chapter 16

"I want us to go out more." He runs his hand over my leg. "I love this but I want to do things with you."

"We just did a bunch of things I really like doing with you." I breathe the words into his chest.

"I liked every one of those things."

After Ben and I had made love, I'd fallen asleep in his arms. He'd woken me shortly after three when his tongue lapped over my folds. I'd held tight to his hair in the darkness as I rode his face into another climax.

I'd drifted back to sleep after that only to be awoken by his erect cock tracing a path over my lips. I greedily accepted it, pulling his desire into me after he'd fucked my mouth at dawn. I slept in his arms the entire night but feel more exhausted now than I did when I first closed my eyes.

"Do you have to work today?" I snuggle into his side, pulling my arms around his waist. "I wish we could both skip work sometimes and spend the day in bed."

"It's hard for me to do that." His hand strokes my forehead. "I can take a day off after I get back from Boston and we can spend it at my place."

"I'd like that." I would. I'd love that in fact. It's becoming harder and harder to pull myself from his arms in the morning to shower and get ready for work. Our schedules don't sync up as well as I'd like but that's part of dating a doctor. I'm quickly learning that. I take his time as it's offered, knowing that when he is with me, all of his attention is focused completely on what's going on between us.

"Are you worried about Noah seeing us together?"

The question slaps me across the face. I've done well with avoiding any questions about Noah for weeks now. Any time his brother's name did fall into the conversation it was related to the wedding. I hadn't brought up the fact that I'd seen Noah at all. Now, lying naked in Ben's arms I feel a sense of betrayal.

I shake my head against his chest. "I don't care if Noah sees us together." It's my truth. I don't care at this point. Noah knows how I feel. I've explained it to him. He knows that I have no intention of ending my relationship with Ben.

"You don't care?"

I can't tell if there's genuine surprise in his question or not. "No, Ben. I don't care. Noah has to accept this."

He sighs heavily enough that my body moves from the motion of his. "You're not worried that he'll go off the rails again and tell you what a fucked up excuse of a man I am?"

Ben is softer than Noah. His soul isn't as jaded and on guard as his. "I know you." I tap my hand against his chest. "I know what's inside of here. You're a good man."

His hand catches mine. "You don't know how scared I was after Noah and Alexa were at my apartment that night."

I do know. I was just as scared. I'd already started falling for Ben at that point and Noah's pointed accusations had made me question everything I knew about him. If I would have listened to his angry words then, I never would be in Ben's bed now. "They were just trying to protect me."

"They care about you a lot. I saw it then."

There was no masking it that night. The heated words and the need to pull me out of Ben's apartment was evidence enough of how much both Alexa and Noah worried about my safety. "They thought they were protecting me."

"I'd never hurt you, " he says the words softly. They're completely unnecessary. I know, without question, that Ben would never do anything that would cause me harm. I have even more faith in that belief since Noah told me about what happened in his hospital room. I still feel my emotions running on high speed whenever I think about Ben standing in silence while his brother beat him.

"I know, Ben." I graze my lips over his chest. "I feel safer with you than I ever have before."

"I want you to always feel that, Kayla."

"I will, " I say it with every promise that the words hold. "I will."

Chapter 17

"There are things I need to tell Ben and Alexa before I get married."

I'm doing it again. I'm meeting Noah in a public place while trying to hide everything from the people I care about. If this is what it feels like to have an affair, I know that's never something I'm going to do. I already feel like shit keeping these meetings from Ben and Lex.

"What things?" I ask because I deserve to know. I've been following Noah through a confusing maze of discovery the past few weeks. I've listened as he's confessed to misjudging his brother and I've been witness to him breaking down from guilt or maybe just the weight of the hatred he's been carrying inside of him for more than a decade.

His eyes float past my face before they settle on some children racing towards a set of swings. We're sitting on a bench at the edge of a park in Brooklyn. I had to deliver a package to a client for Vivian and Noah was doing a child's portrait in the neighborhood. Meeting here seemed like the logical thing to do.

"I should tell you about Sammy."

You should, Noah. You really fucking should.

"I've been wondering about her." That's not true. It's been more than wonder. I'd searched the alumni of Noah and Ben's high school website looking for anything I could find about a woman named Samantha or Sammy. Student records were protected and since it was obvious that she didn't play any sports or participate in any clubs, her name was nowhere to be found. More than once I was tempted to ask Ben about her, but I wanted to have something more substantial before I jumped into that conversation with him. Right now, my only place to navigate from is that she was Ben's first lover and Noah obviously knew her.

"Sammy was my girlfriend."

"What?" The volume of that one word is a clear reflection of what I'm feeling inside. Two women sitting on a bench near us crane their necks to see what I'm screaming about.

He looks down at me. "You're surprised."

What was your first clue, Noah?

"The Samantha Ben slept with that day was your girlfriend?"

"Technically she was my ex-girlfriend when they were together in the guesthouse." He takes a deep drink from the water bottle in his hand. "Or we were on the verge of breaking up."

I'm not sure how to respond. I'm slightly confused about why Ben left out that detail when he was telling me about that day. I can only assume that it's because he was embarrassed that he slept with a woman who was involved with his brother. "I had no idea."

"I met Sammy during my senior year of high school." He stares straight ahead. "She was a party girl. She was already in college. At the time she seemed out of my reach so I chased her until…"

"I understand," I cut him off. I don't want to hear it. I don't need to.

"We partied for weeks. We'd smoke weed and then spend hours at her place. She was a total freak."

I feel the muscles in my stomach knotting. "How did she end up with Ben?"

"Things between her and I started to fall apart right around graduation. She wanted me to take her to senior prom and I wouldn't." He pushes the water bottle against his thigh, smoothing out the fabric of his jeans. "I wouldn't take her anywhere. I was embarrassed."

"Embarrassed of her?"

His hand jumps to his forehead, his index finger scratching his hairline. "Maybe it was her. Ben was dating the perfect girl. She was smart, sweet, and beautiful. He was always talking about how perfect she was. He spent a lot of time at her house helping her parents with odd jobs. I was dating a girl who was on the verge of dropping out of school. Her entire life consisted of getting high and getting fucked."

I cringe at the words. "So you broke it off?"

"That would have been the right thing to do." He bites his bottom lip. "I wasn't into doing the right thing back then. I just stopped talking to her."

"What do you mean?"

"I ignored her. I hooked up with other girls. I just pretended she didn't exist anymore." His tone is cold. "I was such a fucked up asshole."

"You were a teenager," I say, not to assuage his guilt but to move him past it so he'll tell me more about what happened.

"She confronted me in front of my house one day." He rolls the water bottle between his palms. "I didn't want my dad or Ben to see her, so I pushed her into my car and we took off."

"They didn't know you'd broken up?" I'm trying to string the pieces together.

"It wasn't that." His eyes dart over my face in a flash, never settling on my eyes. "I never introduced her to them in the first place. I told them I had a girlfriend but I didn't bring her around."

"I understand." He was ashamed of his choice. I'd felt the same way about some of the boys I dated in high school. I don't think anyone can fault Noah for that.

"We had it out that day." He stares at the ground. "I told her I didn't want anything to do with her. I told her to stay away from me."

"How did she take that?"

A small chuckle pours out of him. "Not well. She told me I couldn't just drop her. She said it wasn't all my decision."

The words bite into a part of me that now feels foreign. I'd thrown some of those same words at Parker when he broke up with me. I may have been older than Sammy was when Noah broke her heart, but the maturity level of the pain was on par. Rejection is a bitter pill for anyone to swallow, regardless of their age. "She was hurt."

"I didn't realize how badly I hurt her," he mutters. "I didn't know until you told me she was the woman Ben was with when our mother died."

Chapter 18

We've sat in silence for the past ten minutes watching children swing and mothers chat. Noah stared off into the distance as I texted with Ben, wishing him a safe trip as he boarded the plane for Boston. I'm grateful that he's away for the next few days. Hearing the details about who Sammy was to Noah has jarred me. I need time to center myself before his brother gets back. I'm eager to talk to him about all of this, but first, I need to hear Noah out.

"How did she end up in bed with Ben?"

He breathes heavily, pulling the air into his lungs. "The day after I told Sammy that I didn't want anything to do with her our mother died."

There's no way the timing is a coincidence. "Why was she at your house?"

"There was a party the night I told her to get lost," he says the words slowly. "It was supposed to be a last hurrah for our graduating class. I'd told her about it weeks before because I wanted her there. I knew Ben wouldn't go. He never partied. He was always studying or hanging out with his girlfriend."

"He went to that party?"

"He did." He nods his head slowly. "His girlfriend was away with her family. She told him to go so he could hang out with his friends. "

"He told me he met Samantha there," I offer even though I'm certain Noah is well aware of every detail.

His hand moves over the edge of the bench, tracing a path along the grain of the wood. "She saw him there. She came on to him. I saw her grinding against him when they were dancing. She was trying to make me jealous."

"Did you tell Ben who she was?"

"I didn't." He looks down at me. "I pulled her outside and told her who he was."

"What did she say?" I cross my legs in an effort to get my body to relax. I feel as though I'm opening a box that contains the key to letting Ben free of all the guilt he's been carrying with him for years.

"She told me that if I wasn't going to fuck her anymore, that she'd fuck him instead."

I push my back into the bench to gain distance from the words. They're harsh. They're almost brutal in their message. "What did you say to her?"

He closes his eyes tightly as he leans forward. "I told her to go right ahead. I said he was second best and always would be."

"She did it to get back at you?"

His mouth thins. "She thought it would hurt me. I didn't take her seriously. I knew Ben was devoted to his girlfriend. They were talking about getting married at some point."

Even though I know that the words were spoken from the mouth of a boy barely old enough to vote they still sting. Thinking about Ben planning a life with a woman he once loved hurts. It also helps place his questions about Parker. He loved a woman the same way I loved him. The promise that first love holds can be so hard to break free from. "What did you say to Ben when you found out about her? When you knew he'd slept with Sammy?"

His eyes rake over my face slowly. I see nothing but intense pain in his gaze. "I've never talked to Ben about it."

"Why?"

"Until you told me that Sammy was the woman he said he was with that day, I thought he was lying, Kayla." His voice is thick and soft. "I thought he was fucking lying about it all."

"About what, Noah?" I reach to grab his arm. "What did you think he was lying about?"

"He wouldn't tell anyone the name of the woman he said he was with that day." He drops his head into his hands. "We all assumed he couldn't give a name because he was lying. My father and I never believed a woman was actually there."

"What?" I bark the word into his face. "Why would he hide the fact that he slept with her?"

"Kayla." He grabs my hand. "My father sat with Ben in the guesthouse for more than an hour before he brought him back to the main house."

I pull on his hand, trying to lodge free all the answers I need. "Just tell me, Noah. Please. None of this is making any sense to me."

"I was alone in that house for so long." His hand is free of mine now and resting against his lips. "I had to call someone."

"Why didn't you just go down to the guesthouse to see Ben?" I already know the answer to that. Noah was fuming with anger over his mother's death. The last thing he wanted was to look at Ben.

"I couldn't do it." He fists his hand against his thigh. "I was in shock. I didn't want to leave my mother's side. I knew the coroner was coming to get her and I couldn't let her go."

"I'm sorry, Noah." I offer to try and center him again. "I'm so sorry you lost her."

"I fucked up so badly, Kayla." His eyes fill with tears. "I've fucked everything up."

"What are you talking about?" I reach to grab his hand again. "Please just tell me."

"When my father brought Ben up to the main house to talk to the police she was already there."

"Your mother was still there?" I try to string together all the disjointed things he's throwing at me. "You were still sitting with your mother then?"

"No." He pants the word out. "No."

"What then?" I'm weighted with so much anxiety I'm fearful my heart is going to stop beating. "Just tell me what was going on in that house."

"Ben walked in. He was clinging to my father. He was crying." Noah's voice cracks as tears start flowing down his cheeks. "He was talking about a woman. He kept saying that she saw him attach the oxygen tank. She was there when he did it and my father could ask her if he wanted. He kept repeating that he was sorry."

I nod. I can picture a younger version of Ben broken from the knowledge that his mother had just died. "He felt so badly, Noah."

"When he finally looked up…" his voice stops. "Kayla, when he finally looked up he stared right at her."

"Who?" I spit the word out.

"I called her over because there was no one else. I couldn't sit there alone anymore."

"Who? Noah tell me who."

"Sammy." He stares right at me. "I fucking called her over to help me deal with my mother's death."

I can't wrap my brain around what he's telling me. None of it fits into what Ben has shared with me. "Samantha was there? Ben saw her with you?"

"I told him she was my girlfriend." He throws his head back and I see the thick vein in his neck pulsing out a beat. "I fucking told my brother that the woman he just lost his virginity to was my fucking girlfriend."

"What did Ben do? What did Sammy say?"

His hands leap to his face. "Ben fell on the floor. He fell on the floor and cried and she just fucking stood there with her mouth shut."

"She didn't tell you about Ben?" I push the question out through a sob. "She didn't tell you she slept with him?"

He turns so swiftly that I almost fall off the side of the bench. "She didn't say a word."

"Why didn't Ben tell you?" It doesn't make sense. All Ben had to do was confess to Noah that he'd slept with Sammy that day. It would have lifted the cloud of uncertainty about his role in his mother's death. It would have given his story the witness that he needed.

"He was trying to protect me." He pulls himself up from the bench. "My little brother was trying to protect my feelings and he ruined his life to do it."

Chapter 19

"You're in Boston?" Alexa's voice carries through my phone. "Why the hell are you there? It's not your family is it? Is someone sick?"

I stare out the window of the taxi I hopped into as soon as I exited the airport. "No." I need to level my voice. "It's not that. I'm here to see a friend."

"You're coming back tomorrow, right?" She pauses. "I mean I need some help with some wedding stuff. I'm flipping out Kayla. There's still a lot to do."

"I'll be there," I say it with conviction. Noah and I had ridden the subway back to my place after our talk. He wanted to see Ben in person and when I told him he was in Boston, we mutually agreed that I should come here to ease Ben into the idea of sitting down for a discussion with Noah. I'm here to do just that. The added bonus of enjoying the look of surprise on his face when he sees me is making my heart beat faster.

"You should pick up your damage deposit while you're there." I can hear the distant tapping of her fingers against something. "I forgot to remind you to call your old landlord last week. Now that you're there in person, you can pick it up."

"That's a great idea, Lex." I stare out the window as we race through the streets of the city I've called home most of my life. "You're tapping your fingers on your desk, aren't you?"

The rhythmic background noise stops. "It's a stressful day. I'm in the school on a Saturday grading papers when I should be out doing things for the wedding."

"Focus on work today, Lex." I breathe deeply. "I'll be back tomorrow and we'll tackle all the wedding stuff as a team. You, me and Sadie."

"Okay." I hear the trepidation in her tone. She's definitely not going to concentrate on anything but whether her special day will go off without a hitch.

"I need to go. I'll call you as soon as I'm back in New York."

"You better." She laughs as she ends the call.

***

"I'm sorry, Ma'am, but you're mistaken." The burly man behind the desk doesn't even look at me as he repeats the same phrase for the third time.

"I don't think I am," I say even though I'm certain that he's right. I've been standing in the lobby of this hotel in downtown Boston for the past ten minutes. This is the third person I've asked about the medical conference that is supposed to be taking place here. Not one of them has any clue about what I'm talking about.

His eyes dart over the counter to peer directly at me. "Let me make a few calls and I'll see if I can locate the right hotel for you."

I nod. I should be more appreciative. I check the log of my text messages again comparing the name of the hotel Ben told me he'd be at to the name on the wall behind the check-in desk. They are definitely one in the same.

I stare down at my phone when I feel it vibrate in my hand.

"Hey, Noah," I say with ease. "How are you?"

"Good." His voice is curt and restrained. "Have you talked to him yet?"

I smile at how eager he is to smooth things over with Ben. It's been what I'd hoped for since I realized the struggle that the two of them have faced all these years. "I just landed an hour ago. I'm at the hotel he said the conference was at, but he's not here."

"Maybe he's at his apartment."

The fact that Ben told me he keeps an apartment in Boston completely slipped my mind. I'm certain that I can track him down there at some point today. "I should call him and tell him I'm here."

"I've got the address if you want it."

"Of course I want it."

***

I feel like I'm chasing a phantom around the streets of Boston. After listening to the desk clerk back at the hotel tell me that he couldn't find any details about a medical conference in the city, I'd left with the address Noah gave me for Ben's place.

It was an upscale condo complex with a doorman who didn't know where to draw the line. The man was a flirt, and given his age,

I'd guess that he had perfected the art of seduction during his very long tenure as the doorman of that building. It took more than forty-five minutes for me to get through a simple series of questions about whether Ben was actually in the building. The overly attentive doorman had spent more time asking me about my past boyfriends than he had telling me where Ben was. At the end of what felt like an awkward date in the lobby of the building, he confessed that Ben hadn't been to the apartment in weeks. He even showed me the stack of mail that he'd been collecting for him.

I'm beginning to question whether I heard him correctly when he said he was coming to Boston. I pull my smartphone out of my purse and call his number. I mutter a curse word under my breath when it goes straight to voicemail. At this point, the excitement of surprising Ben has been replaced with frustration. I leave a short, curt message telling him it's important.

I walk out onto the street, waving for a taxi. I debate sending Ben a text message. I'm not even sure what I'd say.

Instead I slide into the backseat of the first taxi that stops, give the driver the address of where I used to live and stare at my phone, willing Ben to call me back.

Chapter 20

"You owe me that money." I tap my hand against the doorjamb of what my old landlord calls his office. It's actually a small linen closet he has a wooden chair sitting in that faces an old television set.

"I'm not giving you back that money." His eyes don't leave the screen. From the sounds emanating from it, he's watching an old western.

I try to take a step closer to him but there's literally no room to move. "I moved out a long time ago. You actually owe me the full damage deposit plus interest."

He actually spits the tobacco he's been chewing onto the floor at my feet. "You still live there."

The man is living in a different universe than the rest of us. "I live in New York City. I told you I was moving there."

"Your husband still lives there then." Again, with the tobacco. This time he clears my left shoe by no more than a quarter of an inch.

"I don't have a husband." Christ. He must have rented the place to another couple and forgot.

He finally turns to look at me. A grin pulls over his mouth to reveal yellowed, chipped teeth. "Parker. His shit is still up there so move it out. If you do that, I'll give you your cash."

"Why didn't you move it out yourself?" I search aimlessly through my cluttered purse hoping I still have the keys to this apartment. I planned to mail them back after I raced out of Boston in a hurry. I had texted Parker the day I left to tell him to come back to get the few things he'd left behind.

"He's still renting the place." His attention is back on the television. "Your husband gave me checks for a year when you moved in. I cash one a month."

I feel a surge of pleasure knowing that Parker is still paying for the apartment even though he left right before I did. Our deal was simple. I paid the damage deposit, Parker paid the rent and I covered food and incidentals. It seems like I'm at least coming out on top over this.

"I'll be right back with his stuff." I wave the apartment keys in my hand. "Then you'll give me my money?"

"You bet, toots."

I turn on my heel and head straight for the elevator. Maybe this trip to Boston isn't a complete waste of my time.

***

I run my hands along the arm of the suit jacket he wore when he met me at the airport the day I came running back into his arms. He'd planned an entire celebratory day for me. He picked me up after my flight arrived wearing the one and only suit he owned. He drove me to a building we always talked about living in and as we rode up to the roof in the elevator, he'd leaned over and kissed me. All of the hope and promise that I wanted to see in my future was in Parker's kiss that day. I'd held tight to him as we stood on the roof, staring at the sun setting on the city we both loved. We'd made love in the small apartment he was renting and then the next day we found this place. It wasn't much bigger but it was our home. We moved in immediately, charted the course of our life together and then weeks later he stopped loving me.

I move away from the closet and look at the dresser. The apartment had come furnished and we each only had two drawers to store our things in. I open mine and they still sit empty and bare just as they were when I packed up my things and fled the city.

I open Parker's expecting to see the same, but there are black socks and several pairs of boxer briefs neatly folded in the corner. I close the drawer slowly grabbing the pull for the next and sliding it open. T-shirts are sitting there, all folded to the perfection, an outward sign of Parker's incessant need to be organized. I reach to touch one and my hand stops as it grazes over a lump beneath the fabric.

I know I should close it. It's obvious that the landlord was right and Parker is back living here. I'm intruding on his personal space. The right thing to do is to leave my key by the door and walk out before he walks in. I can't stop myself though as images of the life I could have had wash over me in a heated rush. I feel my throat burn as I reach under the t-shirt to pull out a small, square box.

I almost drop it. I know what's inside before I open the lid. My eyes close as they settle on the beautiful solitaire diamond ring that we admired together in the jewelry store window after our first dinner out together when I came back to Boston. I told Parker it was what my dreams were made of and he turned me towards him and whispered that he wanted to make all those dreams come true. He told me then that he couldn't afford the ring. Staring down at in my palm I know that he bought the ring and then broke my heart.

I reach for the side of the dresser to balance not only my feet but also, all of my emotions. I don't know why I came back here. This is my past. Regardless of what hidden treasures lie beneath the cover of Parker's things, the truth came spilling out of his mouth. He didn't want me anymore. I don't want him now. My future is in New York.

I close the box slowly after studying the ring for a minute more. I move the t-shirt aside just as I hear the unmistakable sound of his key in the lock.

This apartment is small. There's no window ledge to stand on like they do in the movies when caught in a space they no longer belong. I belonged here once. This was my home. I just need to walk out there and tell Parker why I'm here. I have to face him. I have to do it. There's no other choice.

I take a step forward when I hear the voices. It's not just one; there are two. Both are male. One is distinctively deeper than the other.

"I want to call her every day." That's Parker. I know his voice. I've known it since we were teenagers desperately in love.

"You can't. We had a deal." I know that voice too. I've heard it before. It's deep and melodic. It's strong.

There's silence and then the shuffle of shoes against the hardwood floor. I inch closer to the doorway of the bedroom. "I wish I hadn't taken the money. She's worth more than that."

Parker took someone's money for something. This isn't a conversation he'd want me to overhear. I have no right to still be listening to this.

"You took it, Parker. You can't undo it."

I reach for the wall to stop myself from falling forward. I'm hearing things now. I know that I am. In my rush to find Ben I forgot to eat anything. I'm lightheaded and my mind is playing tricks on me.

"I want this to be over. I want to know when I can have her back." Parker's voice is strained. I hear the anxiety in it.

"She's getting through to my brother. I've been following her. She's met him a few times now. As soon as he lets me back into his life, she's all yours."

She's all yours.

The words float through my mind as I step into the hallway.

I clear my throat, rest my hand against the wall and stare straight at Parker and Ben as they turn to look at me.

RUIN

Part Three

Chapter 1

His arms are around me before I have time to react. I'd imagined this moment the way women do when their hearts crave to be with the man they once loved. In my dreams, Parker would race through the lobby of my building in New York City, sprint up the stairs and pour his heart out to me the second I opened my apartment door. He'd fall to his knees and tell me that life without me has no meaning and is empty. Now, feeling Parker's strong arms circling my waist, all I feel is numb.

"Kayla." I can sense the smile in his voice, even though his face is buried in my hair. "I can't believe you're here."

"Don't." I push against him, mustering any lingering strength I can find. "Let me go."

"What are you doing here?" His lips press against my temple. "Did you miss me?"

"I heard what you said." I try again, in vain, to shove him away. "I heard you and Ben talking."

He pulls back so harshly I almost lose my footing. "You heard us?"

I turn towards Ben. His face is void of any expression. I can't tell if he's surprised to see me or not. There's no way he could have known that I'd be listening in on his conversation with Parker. He didn't expect me to be here. He thought I was tucked away quietly in New York, planning my best friend's wedding to his brother.

"I can explain what you heard." Parker's hand is on my chin, trying to turn my face towards his. His voice is the same as it's always been, joyous and oblivious to the tribulations that dot other people's lives. Even now, weeks after he'd broken my heart and moments after he inadvertently confessed to taking money from Ben in exchange for avoiding me, he's positive. His tone is a clear indicator that he still believes that everything will be fine, as long as he sees it through rose colored glasses. He expects the pieces of his life to fall into place, regardless of how much pain he causes others to get there.

I can't look at him. I won't make eye contact with him. How is it even possible that these two know each other? "You took his money."

He nods loosely before his eyes flash to Ben and then back to me. "I want you to marry me."

Whoever said that timing is everything couldn't have known how ironic the words can be. "Marry you?" I mimic them back just to hear how utterly ridiculous they sound coming from my own mouth.

"I love you so much. I realize that now." Parker's voice is breaking as he tilts his chin down towards my palm. "I've missed you."

"Shut up," I bark at him, not just because I can't absorb what he's telling me, but also because I feel my stomach lurching with each of his romantic pronouncements. I don't want Parker to love me. I don't want him to tell me he wants to marry me. I wanted that. I ached for that but it's different now.

I twist my head back around to look at Ben. "You gave him money to stay away from me?"

"Kayla." His voice is low, calm and controlled. "We need to go somewhere alone. I need to talk to you in private without Parker."

"No." I shake my head. "We're not going anywhere. You're going to tell me what's going on right here. I want to know right now."

"Baby, you came back to be with me, didn't you?" Parker ignores everything I just said to Ben. "You still love me, right?"

"No." I take a heavy step away from him. "I came here to talk to Ben."

"Ben?" His hand shoots past me, his index finger flying in Ben's direction. "You came to our apartment to talk to Ben?"

"I came to Boston to talk to him," I correct. "I'm not here because of you."

"You're in our apartment, Kayla." There's no disguising the confusion in his tone. "Why are you in our apartment?"

My mind skips back trying to retrace its path. How did I end up here? Why am I standing in the same apartment I shared with Parker mere weeks ago, holding an engagement ring? I pull my hand over my face, glancing down at the small box in my other palm. "I wanted my damage deposit back."

"You what?" His eyes narrow. "You're in our apartment because of the damage deposit?"

It's such a meaningless point right now. I had no idea when I used my key to get back into the home I shared with Parker that my life would splinter into a million pieces inside these walls. "The super said you moved out so I came to clear out your things."

His eyes float down to the box. "You found the engagement ring when you were going through my things?"

I nod, my hand extending out to him. "Take it back. I don't want it."

His blue eyes darken. They look the same as they did the night he left me. "It's your ring, Kayla. It's the one you wanted. I bought it for you."

"No," I whisper so softly that I'm not sure I even said the word. "I don't want it."

He rubs his hands over his face. "I made a mistake when I walked out. I didn't realize how much I loved you then. Give me another chance."

I push the ring into his hand. "I don't want this. I don't want you."

Parker heaves a sigh before the box slips from his hand and drops to the floor. "You can't mean that, baby. You've loved me forever. "

I have. He's right. It felt like he was my forever when I boarded that plane that took me to my new life in New York City a few weeks ago. When Ben had sat down next to me everything changed. The entire course of my life's path had shifted and I'd been swept up in something unfamiliar and exciting. Now, I can't tell if any of that was real or not.

"When did you plan this?" I twist quickly on my heel and face Ben. I take a deep breath, trying to halt a sob. "How long have you known Parker?"

"Forget about him." Parker's breath breezes over my neck as his hands grip my shoulders. "I can explain everything to you."

He can't. He thinks he can but there's no way in hell that Parker can make sense of this riddle that I'm standing in the middle of. "When did you meet Parker? Did you pay him to break up with me, Ben?"

Ben heaves a deep sigh. "I wouldn't do that. I didn't do that. It's not what you think."

"Tell me what it is," I pause long enough to pull myself away from Parker's grasp. "Tell me how this isn't about you paying my boyfriend to stay away from me."

He crosses his arms over his chest. "I'm not discussing this in front of Parker."

"Why not?" I throw the words at him. "You had no trouble discussing me with him a few minutes ago. I heard it all. You're using me to get back in your brother's life."

He shakes his head slightly. "No. I'm not using you to get back Noah."

I feel so deflated. I know what I heard. Ben has been following me. Every time I've met with Noah he was there, somewhere in the background lurking behind the veil of a lie about being busy so he could spy on his brother and me. I need to talk to Noah. I need to tell him that he was right about his brother all along. Ben is manipulative and calculating. He paid Parker to stay away from me and he told him he could have me back as soon as Noah embraced him as family again.

"Kayla." Parker's in front of me now, concern washing over his face. "Please talk to me. Please."

"When did this start?" I look past him to Ben trying to keep my lower lip from trembling. "Tell me when you met Parker."

Ben's gaze narrows on my face as his hand flies to my forearm, pulling it into his grasp. "I need to talk to you in private, Kayla. There are things you need to know."

"Baby, please listen to me." Parker reaches for my other arm, grabbing tightly to my elbow. "I made a mistake when I left you. Let me make it up to you now."

I'm being pulled apart by the two men who have been at the center of my life for the past few months. I can literally feel the energy pouring off each of them. "I just want answers. Someone needs to tell me now what the hell is going on."

"Once Ben leaves I'll explain this all to you." Parker's hand tightens. "This is about us."

It stopped being about us when I went to that hotel room with Ben. "No. This isn't about us, Parker. It's more than that."

"No, it's not." He pulls me towards him. "I fucked up when I left you. I see that now. Let me show you how much I love you."

My eyes flit over Ben's stoic face before they settle on Parker's. "Unless you tell me what the hell is going on between you and Ben, I'm walking out of here."

"I need time alone with her." Parker looks at Ben. "She came here. I didn't ask her to."

I feel my shoulders slump forward with the words. I've become a third party in their game of deceit. Parker's talking about me as if I'm not in the room. Slow tears slide down my cheeks. "Don't do that. Please don't talk about me like I'm not here."

"It's up to Kayla," Ben says with a low growl. "She needs answers. She wants honest answers, Parker. If she wants them from you, so be it."

I follow the line of Parker's sight to Ben's face. He's giving up that easily? He's going to actually walk away and let Parker be my guide through the maze of confusion I'm lost in? That action alone speaks volumes to me.

"I want them from anyone who can give them to me," I interject before Parker has a chance to speak. I push my hand into my lips to quiet the sobs.

"I'm leaving. I don't want you more upset." Ben's hand slides from my forearm to my shoulder. "There are two sides to this, Kayla. I want to explain my side. I'm here until tomorrow for the conference."

"The conference?" I parrot back as I pull free of Parker. I walk towards the door of the apartment with every hope that my knees won't buckle beneath the weight of my emotions. "There is no conference. I was at the hotel you said you'd be at and there was nothing. No one knew about any conference." The righteous indignation in my tone is unmistakable. I admit I'm taking pleasure in pushing Ben into a corner with his lies.

"It's informal. I'm meeting several other doctors in that hotel. You can find me there until five today. It's on the sixth floor in room nineteen." His voice doesn't waver as he offers the pointed details. "After that, I'll be at my condo for the night. I'll text you the address."

"I already have it," I snap back through a muted cry as I turn to face him.

"I'll be waiting to hear from you." His voice is soft as his lips graze my ear. "I know this looks bad, Kayla, but everything I've done is for you."

I swipe at a wayward tear falling down my cheek. This is all so much. Trying to absorb everything that's happened in the last thirty minutes is impossible. "Everything you've done is so you could get Noah back into your life."

"No," he says tightly as he reaches for the doorknob. "This is not about Noah. All I care about is you."

"I'm going to tell him." I glance over my shoulder to where Parker is still standing a few feet away from us. I suddenly wonder how much he knows about the fractured relationship between Ben and his brother. "I'm here in Boston because Noah asked me to talk to you. I have to tell him about this."

His face is impassive as he leans down to brush his lips over my forehead. "Do what you need to do, Kayla. I want you to come out of this in one piece. Do whatever it takes to make that happen. Nothing else matters to me."

Chapter 2

"I think I knew." I reach to grab the arm of the chair before I lower myself down onto the cushion. "It was the only thing that made sense to me, Parker."

He settles on the edge of the matching chair across from me. "I wasn't man enough to tell you at the time. It's not important anymore."

I study his face, soaking in the strong line of his jaw and the curve of his nose. He hasn't changed much since we first met in high school, seven years ago when he was only seventeen. The boyish glint that was always ever present in his eyes is fleeting now. It's lost completely in this moment, replaced by something that mirrors regret. Maybe it's shame or guilt.

I wipe away the last of my tears with the tissue Parker had brought back with him when he went to get me a bottle of water from the kitchen. We'd stood in silence after Ben had left both of us cautiously uncertain of how to begin talking about our failed relationship and what our futures hold.

"Who is she?" It's a question that has been poised at the edge of my tongue since the night he left. Back then, I didn't want to voice my belief that he was leaving me for someone else. He'd worked tirelessly to get me back into his bed in Boston. The notion that he'd throw all of that to the wayside to pursue someone else didn't fit. Now, looking back, I can't be certain that it wasn't just my self-esteem quieting my better judgment. The sensible parts of my heart knew there was someone else. He was too careless with me for it to be anything but that.

"Kayla." He throws his head back with a groan. "Does it even matter anymore? It's over."

He doesn't want it to matter but his decision to leave me for another woman changed my life completely. "I want to know."

"I met her at work." It's a start and judging by the endless pause that follows the words, it's where he wants this discussion to end.

"When?" I ask the question with no emotion. When I was sitting at the gate at the airport weeks ago waiting to board the flight that took me back to New York, I would have given anything for an honest answer to that question. They say that a woman's intuition is never wrong and mine knew, even if I chose to ignore it, that Parker was racing from the bed he shared with me into someone else's.

He scratches the back of his head, his eyes jumping from my face to the wall behind me. "It was before you moved back to Boston."

The words slice through me like a razor sharp edge. "You met her before I came back?"

"Baby," he begins before he leans forward to rest his elbows on his knees. "I was really mixed up back then."

"Did you want her when you begged me to move back to Boston to be with you?" I ask because my mind wants the answer, even if my heart doesn't feel anything when the question leaves my mouth.

He closes his eyes briefly and I see the answer there, in the silent pause. "She had a boyfriend back then."

"You wanted me back because you couldn't have her?" I don't want the question to sound as pathetic as it does. Everything that was scattered and mismatched within my mind for the past few months is now falling into place. "Did you beg me to come back here, Parker, because you were in love with someone you couldn't have?"

"I don't know if I loved her, Kayla," he qualifies. "I liked her and she told me she was involved with another guy."

The weight of his words rolls through me. "You told me you couldn't live without me. You said we were meant to be together."

"We are." He drops swiftly to his knees, his hands darting to my thighs. "I told you I made a mistake. When she broke up with her boyfriend I jumped at the chance to be with her. I thought she really loved me but we fought a lot. She was nothing like you."

He left me for another woman and once he realized she wasn't all fun and frolic, he decided he wanted me back? Is he really confessing that to me right now? "You want me back now because you don't want her?" It's the simplest way to express one of the most complicated questions I've ever asked him.

"Kayla." His chest expands beneath the blue t-shirt he's wearing as he draws a heavy, steady breath. "I chose the wrong woman weeks ago. I should have picked you."

How gracious of him to admit that now. "You left me for her, Parker. Why would I want you back?"

"You loved me the night I left." His eyes sprint over my face. "I saw it when you were crying. You begged me to stay with you."

I'll never forgive myself for that. It's been my deepest regret and I haven't shared it with anyone, not even Alexa. Admitting that I dropped to my knees and literally pulled at the leg of his jeans to get him to stay with me, is something I look back on now with disgust and pain. I never wanted to be that woman. I never wanted my life to be defined by any man and that night I tried desperately to make Parker stay with me. He had shaken me off like a bad habit and hadn't looked back before he slammed the door of this apartment and walked away.

"I wish I could go back to that night," I say the words softly, not wanting to give him any sense of power over me. "I wish I could change the way I acted."

"You acted from your heart." His index finger pats against my hand. "I'll never forget how you looked, Kayla. I've thought about it every day since then."

I've pushed it to the furthest recesses of my mind every day. If I'm being brutally honest with myself it changed who I am on a very fundamental level. It was my rock bottom and for the rest of my life I'll always remember that it was Parker who pushed me there. "I try not to think about it anymore."

"We don't need to." He smiles up at me. "Today is the first day of our new life together. Fate brought you back here, Kayla. We were always meant to be together."

We were never meant to be together. Love isn't supposed to rake you over the coals like this. It's not a game of hide and seek. Parker loves me when it's convenient for him. He's proven that enough times that falling back into the trap that is his empty promises will only stall my life again. I can't do this anymore. I want the answers to my questions and then I want Parker to become a distant memory. "I need some answers, Parker and right now, you're the only person who can give them to me."

"If that's what it's going to take to get you back, ask away."

Chapter 3

I should tell him, right here on the spot, that the chances of the two of us getting back together are level with the chances that I'm going to win the lottery someday. It's never going to happen. I can barely look at him without feeling anger and disgust. The idea of crawling back into a relationship with him is so foreign to me I can't even process it.

"When did you meet Ben?" I ask with quiet resolution. I need a jumping point to clear the hurdle that is his connection to Ben. I heard the fragmented edges of a conversation between the two of them. Now, I want Parker to fill in all those scattered blanks for me.

He leans forward again, tracing his thumb across my knuckles. I don't pull back for fear of losing his desire to do what's right. I know he wants to share with me. I see it in his face. "It wasn't long ago, Kayla."

"How long?" I push because having a full understanding of when they met matters more to me than I'm willing to admit right now. I'm trying to convince myself that I want every single detail so I can carry it all back to Noah when I recount today's events to him. There's more to it than that. I need to know that the night in the hotel room and the days spent with Ben hold some meaning beyond his desperate need to regain Noah's attention.

He pulls his hand through his brown hair, his fingers separating the curly locks. "It was two or three weeks ago."

"Two or three weeks," I repeat back in a mumble. "Where did you meet him? Did he contact you?"

His hand glides from his hair over his face stopping to pinch the bridge of his nose. "I met him outside your apartment building. I was standing on the street when he came out of the building."

"How did you know where to find me?"

He shrugs. "I thought about going to see Alexa to ask her but I didn't want her to rail on me. I thought you might have stayed in touch with your old boss so I stopped by there."

"Vivian told you where I live?" I ask before taking a drink from the bottle of water.

"She said I missed you by twenty minutes." He leans back, smoothing his hands over the front of his shirt. "I had to get up the nerve to talk to you. I stopped at a bar by your place and had a few beers."

I doubt that anything would have turned out differently had I known Parker was only a few feet from the front door of my building just days ago. The fact that he confirmed that he left me for someone else would have come to light then. Seeing his gentle smile would have only been a brief reprieve from the inevitability of it all.

"Once I decided I was ready to talk to you, it was dark out." He glances at his wrist as if he's expecting to find a watch there. "It had to have been near ten. That's when I saw him."

"Ben was outside my building?" There's more surprise woven into the words than I intend. Although our time together was spent mostly in his apartment, he was at my place a few times.

"He almost ran into me when he opened the door." He rolls his eyes. "I was already feeling pretty good from the beers if you know what I mean."

He was bordering on drunk. I don't need him to spell it out for me. When we lived together, Parker would be passed out in bed after two or three beers. "I know," I offer because it's the step I need to take to keep Parker on this path with me. I want him to keep talking so the less I chime in, the better.

"I tried to get into it with him." He rolls his hands into fists and darts them into the air between us. "I was on edge and pissed that he bumped me with the door."

Parker, always the charmer almost hit Ben? "You tried to punch Ben?"

"I egged him on but he just stood there with a smirk on his face."

That sounds exactly like the Ben I've come to know. The idea of him randomly getting in a fistfight with a stranger on the street is foreign to me. I feel a hint of shame wash over me thinking about Parker acting like an asshole. It's misplaced but it's a lingering leftover from all our years together when I had to witness that behavior first hand.

"He said I looked like I could use a beer." His tone is even. "I asked if he was buying and we went back to the bar."

I lock my eyes on his face. "You and Ben drank together at the bar by my place?"

He closes his eyes briefly. "It was for a few hours. He talked about his brother and some chick he was falling for. I wasn't really paying attention."

I don't react. I can't. "What else did he talk about?"

"Nothing. He just listened while I confessed everything to him."

"Confessed what?" I push my hair back behind my ears suddenly feeling very overheated. "What did you tell Ben?"

He hesitates briefly as if he's searching for the right order to place his words. I've seen him do that before. It's a ploy he uses when he wants to soften the emotional blow of whatever he's about to say. He did it repeatedly the night he left me. "It was mostly about her."

"Her?" I don't even know her name. I don't need to know it but he's about to tell me.

"Elsie," he offers softly. "That's the woman I …"

"Yes," I interrupt. I don't want this discussion to jump into a tailspin and rocket off into a direction I don't want it to. "You talked to Ben about her?"

"I told him she left me that day," he begins before he stops himself. "I mean I told Ben that Elsie and I broke up."

I don't care. I truly don't care if Elsie walked out on Parker when he was begging her to stay. I've emotionally left. If I had any doubt about that before tonight, it's all been erased and replaced with a sense of quiet closure.

"I'm sorry, Kayla." He sighs before he continues, "I told Ben that I realized what a mistake I made and that I was in love with the girl I broke up with. I told him I was in New York to ask her to marry me."

"You told Ben that was me?" There's no excitement in the question at all. Right now, they are only empty words that are strung together to get me to the truth of what's going on. I'm still reeling from discovering that Ben has been using me as a pawn to get back into Noah's life. Knowing that he enlisted Parker's help to do that doesn't change anything about the way I feel. I don't want Parker in my life. I certainly don't want to be engaged to him.

"No." He hangs his head down. "I never said your name when we were at the bar. He didn't know it was you."

It's obvious that at some point the two of them realized my connection to them both. "When did Ben know I was the woman you were talking about?"

"I'd say about a week after that."

"A week?" I throw the question at him sharply. "I don't understand how you went from talking about me at a bar to agreeing to take money from him to stay away from me."

"It wasn't like that." His hand trails a path across his lap before it stops short of my knee. I'm grateful that he doesn't try and touch me. I don't know that I could resist the urge to pull back at this point.

"What was it like?"

"Kayla, please try and understand where my mind was back then." His voice is no louder than a whisper. "I just wanted to ask you to marry me so we could start all over. So I could forget what a fucking idiot I'd been before you moved back to New York."

I see the vulnerability in his eyes. I know he's in pain. I know that he wishes that he could undo what happened between us but that's not possible anymore. Life has changed. I've changed. "I want to understand, Parker. I really need to."

His gaze drops to his lap. I watch his shoulders surge forward. "Ben offered to help me that first night at the bar. He didn't know me, Kayla, and he just up and helped me."

"Helped you?" I tilt my chin down hoping he'll catch a glimpse of me out of the corner of his eye. "How did Ben help you?"

He pulls his body back until he's facing me directly. "I told Ben that I wanted to ask the love of my life to marry me."

I work hard to not react to the words. "What did Ben say?"

His palm etches a path over his lips. "It's not what he said, Kayla. It's what he did."

I'm stuck. I want to know. I need to know but I'm scared that Parker is about to tell me that Ben concocted a plan to keep Parker from me because of his selfish agenda to get Noah back. I honestly don't know if I would have taken Parker back if he would have showed up at my apartment door with the beautiful ring I longed for, in his hand, and a marriage proposal on his lips. The idealistic part of me wants to believe I would have turned him down, but the romantic parts of my heart, know better.

"What did he do, Parker?" I ask for clarity, not for me, but for Parker. I want him to know that I need to know this. It is instrumental to my moving forward with my life. I have to sort out what happened between these two men before I can even think about talking to Noah and Alexa about this.

"He told me he believed in true love." He cocks his head to the side. "He said young love was worth fighting for."

It sounds like something Ben would say. His soul is soft and hopeful. I saw it myself when he cared for me after my fall. The man that tended to my wounds and nursed me back to health is so opposite of the man who I heard talking to Parker hours ago. They don't fit together, regardless of what my heart is still hoping for.

"I told him I had to go back to my hotel to sleep before I went to see my girl." His index finger taps my knee. "He told me we needed to make a stop first. He was feeling good too but he wasn't as drunk as me."

I look away to steel my emotions. Knowing that the man that I loved for years was getting drunk in a bar with the man I was beginning to fall for is already a lot to absorb. "Where did he take you?"

"To the bank, Kayla," he says in a rush. "We went to the automated teller machine."

"What? Why?" I spit the questions out so quickly they are almost indistinguishable from one another.

"He took out three thousand dollars and handed it all to me," he says hoarsely. "He said it was for the ring. He wanted me to get it so I could ask the woman I love to marry me."

My emotions swing to the side as if they've been slapped. "Ben just handed you the money to buy that ring?"

He drops his head into his hands. "I took it. I took his number too so I could pay him back but he told me it was his gift. He said he wanted to help make Elsie's dreams come true."

Chapter 4

This is what it must feel like to be driving in the middle of a fog patch. You know that you're headed in the right direction but beyond that, everything is murky and hard to place. I need Parker to explain more to me but hearing him tell me that Ben gave him the money for the ring has stalled everything in my mind.

"You said that Ben told you to make Elsie's dreams come true?" I want Parker to repeat it back to me. It doesn't add up.

He scrubs his hand over his face. "I didn't realize he used her name until the next morning when I woke up and thought about what had happened. I sent him a text message telling him I'd pay him back when I could and he replied saying that knowing Elsie would be happy was enough for him."

"Why would he think the ring was for her?" My eyes drop to the floor where the wayward ring box still sits. Parker never bent down to pick it up and I never offered to retrieve it either. It holds absolutely no meaning to me now. He may as well give it to Elsie.

"I was all over the place in the bar." He runs both his hands through this hair, pushing the curls back from his forehead. "I guess he just assumed that Elsie was the one I wanted."

She was. He wanted her enough to leave me only a few weeks ago. Parker wasn't kidding when he said he was all over the place. He still is. He's adrift emotionally and looking for anyone who can give him an anchor. I know that's the only reason he wants to marry me. It's because she dumped him. Being alone is torture to him.

"You corrected him at some point I'm guessing." I'm not really guessing. I know he did. The conversation they shared when they walked into his apartment is proof of that.

"I called him again about a week after that." He licks his upper lip. "I felt guilty about the money so I told him I wanted to work out a repayment plan."

"That makes sense." It does. Parker is proud. He's always been too proud to go to his wealthy family and ask them for any help at all. The fact that he took money from a stranger to buy a ring is shocking. The fact that he wanted to pay it back isn't surprising in the least.

"That's when I corrected him and told him the woman I loved was named Kayla."

I stare at him, my lips slightly ajar. I want to say something that will halt this in its tracks now. I don't want to know any details beyond this because it's when everything shifts to something more sinister. It's the point where Ben transforms from the helpful, kind and caring stranger to the man who used Parker and me to try and get his brother back.

"Did he tell you that he knew me then?" I ask quietly.

His jaw tenses slightly. "He said he was actually coming out of your apartment that night we met. He said you knew his brother, Noah. I asked if it was Alexa's Noah and he said it was. I realized then that's how you met him. It was through them."

"What else did he say?" Judging by Parker's lack of response to Ben's kiss on my forehead earlier he hasn't connected the dots enough to know that Ben and I are lovers. I'm not going to change that by correcting him about the details of how I met Ben.

"He said you were a good person." A small smile pulls at the corner of his mouth. "I said I already knew that."

"What else?" I push through the pleasantries. I need to.

His eyes move over my face. "He said that you were helping him accept some stuff that happened between him and his brother a long time ago. I didn't ask for the details."

I'm grateful for that. What happened between Noah and Ben when they were teenagers isn't Parker's business. Pulling him into that circle of information isn't something I'd ever do. Ben and Noah's pain is theirs alone to share with who they choose. "Ben said that you had a deal?"

"We did." He nods only slightly as if he doesn't want to fully acknowledge it. "Ben told me to keep the money for the ring. He said he just needed more time with you to help him deal with what happened between him and Noah. He said you were the best friend he's ever had."

Those words should buoy my heart. I know, judging by the routine of Ben's life that he doesn't have close friends he confides in. Work is his focus. It's how he shoulders the burdens of his past. "You agreed to give him that time with me?"

"I did." He pinches the bridge of his nose. "I thought you could help him while I worked on finding a new place for us to live."

My eyes take in the room. This apartment had been my safe place for a few months before I'd been thrown back into the sea of uncertainty that Parker had tossed me into when he left me. I imagined we'd build our lives together in this place and now all I see when I look around is emptiness and what could have been.

"Today you told Ben you wanted to talk to me," I say the words evenly. I'm not bringing it up because I want to know what Parker was going to say if Ben would have given him the green light. I'm sure it would have included a marriage proposal and the promise of a future that would have lasted only a few months until someone else caught Parker's eager and willing eye.

"A few days ago I called him and told him I wanted to talk to you." His expression is as vacant as I feel right now. "I just wanted to know if you still wanted me."

I don't delve into that pool because I'd have to tell Parker the truth, which is that I stopped wanting him weeks ago. "He wouldn't let you talk to me?"

"He told me he was coming to town this weekend and we'd talk then." He shrugs.

It stings even though it shouldn't. The mere fact that Parker gave up on talking to me so easily only bolsters my belief that we were never really meant to be. "That's what was going on when I overheard you."

His lips thin into grimace. "I shouldn't have agreed to what he wanted, Kayla. I should have come right back to New York to ask you to marry me but I've been so nervous about how you'd react that I kept putting it off. He kept telling me to take time to think things through. He said he didn't think I was over Elsie yet. I was really confused. Now everything is all fucked up."

"Everything works out the way it's supposed to, Parker," I offer as I pull myself to my feet. "It wouldn't have worked between us anyway."

"Why not?" He doesn't move from where he's seated.

"I don't love you anymore." I look directly at his face as the words leave my lips. "It's over for me. It ended the night you left me for her."

He doesn't respond. I see nothing within his expression so I turn on my heels, walk across the apartment and out of Parker's life for good.

Chapter 5

"What time are you done for the day?" His deep voice jars me out of the number coma I've been stuck in for much of the afternoon. I wish I could say that I was doing something fascinating like working out the details of a big merger, or planning out the investment strategy of a client, but I'm balancing Vivian's checkbook for her. Yes, this is the life of a single, accomplished woman in Manhattan.

"Noah." I grip the side of my desk to calm my shaking hands. I'd been avoiding his texts since they started to roll in on Saturday evening shortly after I left Parker's apartment. I sent him back one, brief response, early Sunday morning after I'd been woken up by a loud argument in the room next to me in a hotel I stayed at. I'd debated calling my mother to see if I could crash in my old room but the price for that would have been too steep. Answering questions about Parker and me, and my time in Boston was too much for me to handle at the time. It's too much to bear now.

"We need to talk." There's urgency in his words.

I glance at the clock on the wall behind his head. It's after six. I can leave any time after four but on this Monday, the mindless haze of doing anything but sitting in my apartment has been my goal. I have to face my reality, in the form of Noah, now. "I can leave now."

"Let's go downstairs to the diner." He motions towards my office door. "I'll buy you an early dinner."

The thought of food itself is enough to make my stomach recoil. I haven't eaten more than a few bites of an apple since I woke up yesterday. Food, sleep and functioning normally are all out of my reach. "I'll just watch you eat."

"You'll eat." His hand grazes over my shoulder as I walk next to him towards the bank of elevators. The offices are silent. Vivian and everyone else left for the day with quiet goodbyes hours ago. I know they could sense I wasn't in the mood for idle chitchat.

"I'm not hungry." Arguing such an unimportant point seems futile. I know Noah well enough to know that it's easier to acquiesce to what he wants, especially if it's something this mundane.

He looks down at me, his eyes raking over my face. "You look tired. Did you sleep last night?"

Normally if a man made a remark like that, I'd be offended but I've seen what I look like in the mirror. I hadn't slept. I had replayed my time in Parker's apartment over and over again in my mind all last night. I haven't spoken to him or Ben since. I'm not sure I ever will again. "I didn't sleep much."

"You'll sleep better tonight." His hand is on my lower back as he steers me into the elevator car. "We have a lot to talk about."

He's right. We do. I have to tell him that even though I've spent weeks trying to convince him that Ben is a good person, that I was wrong. I have to tell him that I gave him false hope right before his wedding to Alexa. I have to confess that I was blinded by Ben's charm and sensual persuasion. To put it simply, I have to admit that I fucked up royally and pulled both him and Alexa right into the heart of the mess.

We ride the elevator in silence before I follow him through the lobby of the building and out into the streets of lower Manhattan. Working in a building on Wall Street fueled me when I first came to this city months ago, but now, since I've returned post Parker break-up, I've felt out of place. The people who work here are in control of their lives. I don't belong here. I don't belong in Boston anymore either.

"There's a place down the street we can eat at." He motions to the left and I nod.

I feel as though I'm a pirate walking the plank for stealing a bounty that never belonged to her. I took things from Noah that I shouldn't have. I exposed fragments of him that he wanted hidden. I saw the vulnerable parts of his heart that are only reserved for Alexa.

We enter the bustling eatery and instantly I'm assaulted with the rumbling din of the crowd in the small space. I wish I had insisted on Noah taking me home. At least there, I can find my center enough that I can confess without having to raise my voice just to be heard.

"Over there." He gestures towards an empty table near the back of the eatery. It's small and pushed into a corner but at the very least it will offer some solace from the noise. I follow him, running the first words that I want to say to him through my mind. I want to soften the blow if that's even possible.

"I've never been here," I say quietly as we sit next to each other. I haven't. I typically don't eat more for lunch than a piece of fruit or a salad I've brought from home. I've heard about the homemade soup here from Vivian. I know, without a doubt, that if they didn't deliver, I'd be racing down here on a daily basis to grab her lunch for her.

"You only sent me back one text when you were in Boston." His eyes search the expansive menu. "I was worried about you."

I'm touched by his concern. Before I left for Boston he'd confided that he liked hanging out with me. I felt as though we were finding our way into a trusted friendship. It meant a lot at the time because of our combined connections of Alexa and Ben. Now, I feel like a fraud for still wanting that. I don't have any close friends beyond Alexa. Having Noah in my corner too meant more than I was willing to admit to him or to myself.

The waitress appears out of nowhere rattling off an impressive list of daily specials. I opt for the soup of the day and Noah settles on a fish and chips platter. After taking our orders, she's gone back into the crowd in a flash.

"Your ex-boyfriend is an asshole."

My eyes jump from the worn and chipped wooden table to his face. "What did you just say?"

"That guy, Parker, he's an ass." He cocks a brow as if he's waiting for confirmation.

Alexa must have told him about my break up and now he's assuming that I saw Parker when I was in Boston. It's an assumption anyone would leap to. I can't deny that if Ben wasn't in the picture, and I wasn't in search of my long lost damage deposit, that I wouldn't have wanted to meet up with Parker. I needed the closure last Saturday had given me. I just hadn't realized it until I walked out of his apartment.

"He's an ass, yes," I confirm with a sly smile. "I'm not sure what I ever saw in him."

"Happiness," he offers as he takes a sip of the water in front of him. "You moved back to Boston to be with him a few months ago. You must have cared a lot about him."

"I did." There's a bite of pleasure as I use the past tense. "I don't care about him anymore."

His eyes waft over the table next to us before they settle back on my face. "I'm glad. He really hurt you."

"Alexa told you how he left me." I can't meet his eyes. I'm afraid I'll cry. I thought I was over the pain of Saturday, but now, talking about Parker again has brought everything that I heard between him and Ben back to the surface.

I sense him moving forward as I hear the table creak beneath the weight of his elbows. "Alexa didn't tell me, Kayla. Ben did."

Chapter 6

I opened my mouth to respond just as the waitress showed up with our food. It's a diner. I should have expected that it wouldn't take more than a couple of minutes for her to return. The entire philosophy of the place is fast food. I take one look at the murky darkness of my soup and decide that my stomach will thank me later if I don't indulge. Noah dives into his food with full force, taking mouthful after mouthful with barely a chew in between. His mannerisms almost match Ben's each movement, as he ate lunch in front of me in a bistro not more than a few weeks ago.

"I saw Ben yesterday," he says as he swallows. "He asked Ron to arrange it."

I take a deep breath to rein in my crumbling emotions. I had no idea. There's no way I could have known that Noah and Ben spoke. The last I heard Noah was open to giving Ben another chance. I was actually in route to arrange a meeting between them when I'd been sidetracked by the overheard confessions of Ben and Parker. "Your father arranged it?" I ask in a quiet voice.

"He said Ben called him from Boston on Saturday night. He was torn up about you and about me." He cocks a brow. "He told Ron it was urgent that he speak to me."

"That's why you texted me so many times," I whisper as much into the air between us as at Noah.

"I texted you more than twenty times, Kayla." He sighs audibly. "I wanted to know what happened in Boston. I wanted to know what you told Ben about me before I saw him."

The answer to that is simple. "Nothing, Noah. We never got around to talking about you other than..." my voice trails. This is where I'm supposed to tell Noah that Ben was following me to watch our secret meetings.

"Other than what?" He leans forward waiting for me to respond.

"I heard him say something to Parker about you," I begin because it's where I need to start emotionally. I'm not going to throw Ben's devious behavior in Noah's face without some warning to soften it.

He motions towards me with his fork. "Ben told me about that. Christ, that's fucked up, Kayla."

It's all fucked up. All of it is. Even this part of it where I'm sitting in a diner listening to Noah tell me that he knows more about my situation than I ever wanted him to. I'm humiliated that I cared for Ben. I'm ashamed that I gave my heart to Parker and I'm hopeful that I can escape this dinner with some of my dignity still in place.

I only nod in response because trying to find words to express how I've messed up my life isn't possible right now.

He wipes the paper napkin over his lips before he places his large hands on the table. "Ben followed you twice when you and I met."

"I know." My eyes dart from his face to his hands. I didn't know that it was only twice but considering the fact that Noah and I only met a few times, it makes perfect sense.

He smiles but it's fleeting and within a blink of my eye it's vanished. "So you know why he followed you?"

I know that Noah likes to draw people out of their shells without revealing too much of himself. Whether he's consciously aware of it or not, he's doing that to me now. I just want him to tell me what he discussed with Ben. "He wanted to see whether I was getting through to you, I guess," I say it stiffly. "He was using me to try and reconnect with you."

"Who told you that? Ben or Parker?" His head tilts to the right. "Which one told you that?"

"Ben said it when I heard them talking," I begin and then stop to take a drink of water. I dart my tongue over my bottom lip before I continue, "I heard Ben say that he followed me and that he could tell I was getting through to you and…" I stop again because confessing to Noah that Ben was going to hand me back to Parker on a silver platter once he and Noah were on better terms, stings too much.

"Ben told Parker you were his again when he got me back." Noah's eyes meet mine and I see a soft understanding there. He knows so much more than I thought he did. Judging by what he's told me so far, Ben has shared almost every detail of the exchange in Parker's apartment with him. "He only said those things to keep that asshole away from you. He knew Parker was a son-of-bitch."

I catch my breath to hold back an unexpected sob. I shouldn't be surprised that I'm this emotional. I've been holding everything in for two days. I wanted to cry when I'd checked myself into the small hotel room in Boston but as I sat in the bathtub there for more than an hour, nothing came. I was numb. I am numb. I've been that way since I heard Ben and Parker talking about me.

Noah reaches across the table to grab my hand. "You should have called me, Kayla. I would have come there. Alexa and I would have been on the next flight to come get you."

The words touch me so deeply that I weep aloud. "I didn't know that."

"We are your family." His large hand cradles mine tenderly. "We will always be your family. Tell me you know that."

I nod without raising my gaze from my lap. "I do know that, Noah."

"We need to talk about Ben, Kayla." His tone is smooth and direct. "I need to explain what's really going on."

I want someone to. I need someone to and if that someone is Noah Foster, I'm all ears.

Chapter 7

"I didn't choose Sadie to be my matron-of-honor because I love her more than you." Alexa sits down on the edge of the bed in the guestroom of the apartment she shares with Noah.

He'd brought me back here in a cab after we'd finished our dinner. It was important to him that Alexa be part of our conversation. She'd insisted that I spend the night at their place after he called to tell her he was bringing me over. I was grateful for the chance to sleep in this bed again. I feel safe here and a part of something that matters. I feel truly as though I'm with family.

"Sadie and you are so different," she continues without waiting for me to respond. "She needs me in ways you don't, Kayla."

"I know that she does, Lex." I reach for her hand. "You've known her a lot longer than you've known me."

"That's part of it, I guess." She twirls her index finger over the fingernail of my thumb. "It's more about how strong you are. I admire that about you."

She's never shared that with me. We've complimented each other the way close friends do when one is feeling battered by the world. I did it when she had her heart broken in Paris by Beck, an artist who had swept her off her feet and into his bed. She'd done it for me when I was passed over for an internship during my junior year of college. She was ready to march down to the office of the company I wanted a placement with to give them a speech about why they were making a mistake they'd regret. We've always had each other's backs. It goes without saying.

"Noah told me about what happened at your apartment in Boston the other day." Her hands leap in unison to her chest. "Kayla…" her voice stalls as tears fill her eyes.

"No, Lex, don't." I reach up to cover her hands with my own. "I was okay. I handled it."

She shakes her head from side-to-side so violently her earrings crash softly against her neck. "You were there all alone after that. I would have come. You should have called me."

"I needed time to process it all," I say quietly. I really did. I needed the silent solace that my own company brought me. I needed that yesterday too. That's why I turned off my phone before I headed back to the airport and I didn't turn it back on until this morning. I wanted my own selfish way to escape the overwhelming pain I was feeling after listening to Parker and Ben talk about me.

"Noah is waiting for us in the other room." She stands and runs her hands over the smooth lines of her pencil skirt. "We'll help you through this together."

I take her outstretched hand in mine, pull myself off the bed and follow her towards the understanding I need.

***

"Ben told you that?" I inch forward on the edge of the comfortable leather chair I sat in when Alexa and I joined Noah in their expansive living room.

Noah leans back, his arm resting on the back of the couch behind Alexa. "He said it."

"Do you think he meant it?" I'm not sure where the question comes from other than a curious need to know. Noah isn't the person to ask about the intention behind Ben's words. The two haven't spoken more than a few times in the past decade. The fact that they spent more than an hour together yesterday isn't helping me in my belief that Noah doesn't know Ben much better than I do.

He looks at Alexa before he pulls his gaze back to my face. "I think he meant it."

"Ben actually told you he cared that much about me?" I'm mincing words because repeating back what Noah just said to me is overwhelming.

He moves Alexa's hair back from her face before he runs his finger over her cheek. "Ben told me that he's never been in love, Kayla. He told me that he's feeling things for you he's never felt for any woman before."

It's impacting me in a way I don't want it to. "Noah…I mean, Alexa…" I stammer, trying to find a starting point. "When you found out that I was seeing Ben, you told me he wasn't good for me."

"Noah did say that," Alexa jumps in as she rests her hand on his thigh. "Things have changed since then."

"I've only ever been in love once," I offer as much to remind myself as them. "Parker's love was toxic. I never really mattered to him. I think I was just filling in his time. I was his go-to when no one else wanted him."

Alexa's bottom lip quivers as she listens intently to what I'm saying. Sympathy isn't my end goal. I don't want that from either of them. I'm done feeling sorry for myself too, but I'm cautious. I have to be. If I jump off the cliff of uncertainty that I'm perched on and fall into the belief that Ben is feeling intense things for me, I'm just setting myself up for another emotional fall. I can't do that. I'm still nursing the wounds Parker gave me.

"I think Parker loved you, Kayla." Alexa leans forward a bit to make her point. "I think he really wanted you back when he asked you to move back to Boston."

"It doesn't matter anymore," I say it with a small smile. "I know that Parker is my past. I also know that I heard things that he said to Ben and I still don't understand it all."

"Kayla." Noah grabs tightly to Alexa's hand, pulling it into his lap. "Ben explained all of that to me."

"Tell me," I push quickly. "I want to understand it, Noah. I need to."

He nods before his eyes dart to Alexa's. "Parker was caught up in something with some girl named, Elsie."

It's still only been two days since I first heard Parker share her name with me. Hearing it come from Noah's lips is surreal. "Ben told you that?"

His jaws tenses. "He said that Parker talked about her non-stop for hours the first night they met. They hung out at a bar by your place getting wasted together."

"I still can't believe they met on the street in front of my place." I don't mention it for any reason other than to reiterate what I've been feeling internally. "Ben didn't come over to my place a lot."

"Ben said he left your place that night because you wanted to tell Alexa about him and he freaked. He thought he'd lose you right then."

"It was that night?" I cock a brow. "That was the night Ben and Parker met?" I remember the night vividly. We'd made love in my bed and then I'd pushed him to tell Noah about us. He'd refused and in my desperate need to stop hiding my relationship with him, I'd told him that unless he did it, I was going to Alexa to tell her everything. He'd run out of my apartment after that and apparently right into Parker.

"He said he needed a drink and Parker looked like he could use a friend so they went to the bar together." Noah crosses his long legs. "That's when Parker started talking about Elsie."

"I'm sorry, Kayla." Alexa leans forward. "We don't have to talk about her if it's too much."

"It's fine," I say with my eyes closed. It has to be fine. It's my reality. "Parker told me all about her."

"I can't believe he asked her to marry him."

My eyes pop open at Alexa's words. In the big picture of my messed up life, there's very little reason to correct her but my need to hold onto any lingering bit of pride that I have wins out. "Parker told me that there was some confusion about that. Apparently Ben thought Parker wanted to marry Elsie, but it was me he wanted to marry."

Her eyes shoot so quickly to Noah's face that I don't get a chance to see anything within her expression. He nods slowly at her as if to encourage her to share something that she's unwilling to let go of.

"Alexa?" I whisper her name wanting her to turn and look at me again. "Lex, what's wrong?"

"Parker didn't buy that ring for you, Kayla." She pushes a puff of air out between her lips to curb her emotions. "He bought it for Elsie but she turned him down."

Chapter 8

It was inevitable that I'd end up back here. It's the third time today that I've stood on the street in front of his building. I should have gone to the hospital but I don't trust myself to keep it together when I see him. The things I want to say to him aren't meant for others to hear.

"Kayla?" His voice is behind me. It rises above the noise of the pedestrian traffic that is filling the late afternoon air. "Is that you?"

I turn quickly to face him. It's only been a few days since I saw him in Boston but he looks different. He hasn't shaved and the beard that covers his jaw makes him look less polished and put together. He actually looks more like Noah today.

"You look flushed." His hand leaps to my cheek. "Are you feeling okay?"

I nod slowly even though the gesture itself is a lie. I'm not okay. I haven't been okay since Noah told me about all the text messages that Ben had shown him on his phone. Text messages that he'd shared with Parker about me, and about Elsie. They emphasized everything Noah and Alexa had told me.

"You've spoken to Noah, haven't you?" His hand moves to my shoulder. "Do you want to come up to talk?"

I only nod again because I'm fearful that if I open my mouth at this point, the only thing that will escape it is a whimper.

He guides me through the lobby of his building before he jabs his index finger into the elevator call button. He makes small talk with a couple who exit the lift when it pops open. I dart around them wanting to avoid the meaningless chatter.

He reaches to cup my hand in his after he presses the button for his floor. He doesn't say a word to the man who raced to get into the elevator before the doors closed. I'm grateful for the silence. It's helping me sort through my tangled thoughts. I watch the lights on the control panel bounce around as the car starts and stops on three floors before we reach our destination.

"I just need to call the hospital once we're inside." He fumbles with his keys as he holds firmly to my hand. "I'll make it quick."

"Take your time," I offer back as we step over the threshold into his apartment. My chest tightens as I take in the now familiar place. I didn't think I'd ever be back here after hearing him school Parker on the details of their supposed agreement. Now, I'm staring at the desk where he fucked me senseless within moments of my arrival one night. This is the place where I started to fall for him.

"I just need to check on a patient I admitted a couple of hours ago." He kisses my hand before he lets it fall to my side. "She wasn't being cooperative when I left. I want to make certain she's doing better."

Of course he does. It's who he is inside. It's that natural need of his to take care of everyone in the world but himself. "I'll wait in the other room for you."

"This won't take long," he calls over his shoulder as he dashes down the hallway.

I walk through the foyer into the large living room. I settle down on the couch and pull my phone from my purse. I run my thumb over the screen, reading a brief text message Alexa sent me earlier about the final fitting on my bridesmaid dress. With my own life being in freefall mode the past few days, I'd forgotten her wedding. The barrage of short text messages she's been sending me all day reminding me to help her with the ever present details of her to-do list, have jarred me back to the reality of honoring my commitment to help make her special day with Noah as perfect as it can possibly be.

I tap out a response telling her I'll be at the dress shop on time tomorrow after I'm done at work. I scroll through my other messages before noticing one from Parker. I delete it without reading it. I won't open myself up to him again. Parker's promises hold no weight for me.

"I'm sorry I had to do that." Ben's voice calls to me from the edge of the hallway. "Work is never ending for me."

I stare at him as he enters the space. The arms of his dress shirt are rolled unevenly and pushed up above his elbows, showing off the firmness of his forearms. His navy pants are wrinkled and the belt's end hangs loose. At first glance he looks disheveled and careless but I know it's only a reflection of his commitment to his patients. He's worked hard today. The evidence is there in the tightness of his jaw and the wrinkle of his brow. He's concerned and he's anxious and his need to call the hospital so soon after leaving there is proof that being a doctor is more than his job. It's an integral part of him, just as much as being Noah's brother is.

"Sit with me," I whisper as I pat the cushion next to me. "Please, Ben."

He's there in an instant, tossing his phone on the table as he lowers himself next to me. He pulls my hand back into his before he closes his eyes and brings it to his mouth. "Thank you for coming here, Kayla. Thank you."

Chapter 9

"There are so many of them." I can't pull my eyes from the screen of his smartphone. "Noah told me a little about it, but he didn't say it was like this."

One of Ben's hands rests on my thigh while the other is cast behind me across the back of the sofa. He's leaning so close to me that I can smell the intoxicating scent of his skin. "Noah scrolled through a bunch of them."

I nod slowly. "Why did you keep them all?"

"I kept the first one because I'm bad at clearing out my phone." A small chuckle moves his chest forward a touch. "Once Parker mentioned your name I wanted to have them just in case I ever needed to show you."

I drop the phone to my lap. "You really didn't know who he was when you gave him the money for the ring, did you?" It's a question that I've already found the answer to in the saved messages on his phone. I read Parker's text thanking Ben for the gift.

His brow cocks. "He was just a random guy I had a few drinks with. He seemed down on his luck. I wanted to help him out."

"He's an ass," I mutter beneath my breath. It's an accurate description given the fact that I've just read more than three dozen messages on Ben's phone from Parker. Messages where he tells Ben that he's unsure if he's in love with me or Elsie and messages where he confesses to a split second decision to ask Elsie to marry him the day after he returned to Boston after meeting Ben.

He reaches to take the phone from me. "He's confused. He's not worthy of someone like you."

At any other moment in my life I'd find the words cheesy, but now they are anything but that. "Why didn't you tell me right away? You should have told me you knew Parker."

He places the phone on the cushion next to him before he raises his hand to his brow. He slowly runs it over his forehead. "You're the most amazing person I've ever known."

It's not an answer to my question. I want to push but I can sense from the tension in his shoulders that I need to let him set the pace.

He closes his eyes briefly before his hand juts back to mine. "I've been close to one person in my life."

"Your mother," I offer. It's not a question. It's a fact. I know that is his truth.

"Yes." He tilts his chin down. "When she died I stopped feeling anything."

I've never dealt with a death that profound so the emotional compass I'm operating with in terms of grief is very different than Ben's. I've imagined loss but I don't believe that's the same thing. I know it's not. Since meeting Ben, I've seen the devastating impact that death can have on someone. "I'm sorry you lost her."

"I am too," he says through a heavy sigh. "I went into medicine to heal people. It gave me a focus that I really needed. I can help a lot of people without getting too emotionally attached."

"You care for your patients." I still as I stare at his handsome face.

"I try to stay objective with them." He pops his brows up as he looks at me. "It's not always easy."

I want to know more about that because it's the very essence of who he is. Today is a perfect example of that. When I first turned towards him on the street, I could see the concern in his face. Part of that was directed towards me, but there was more beneath the surface. It's not possible for him to walk away from his work when the clock strikes four the way I do. He carries it with him. It's always there, pulling at him in ways I'll never truly grasp.

"I've only ever really cared for my mother." His eyes soften. "I mean I love my dad and Noah, but it's not the same."

I've never heard him speak openly of his feelings for his brother. It reassures me in some abstract way that I'm doing the right thing by coming to see him. "You've never been in love with a woman?"

The corner of his mouth jets up into a small smile. "No. I've cared for women but it was mostly related to sex. I'd keep my feelings out of it."

I admire the emotional control he has. I'm the exact opposite. Although I haven't ever loved anyone beyond Parker, I've cared deeply for two other men. I felt I could have fallen desperately in love with either but the circumstances never worked out that way. What I feel now, for Ben, is different. I want to express that but it's so jumbled together with the confusion that still lingers from the weekend and our encounter in Boston. I'm not ready to pour my heart out.

"Do you remember when we met on the airplane?"

My eyes dart over his face when he asks the question. "Of course I do, Ben."

"I was sitting in first class when you boarded." He scrubs the back of his neck with his hand. "You walked right past me."

"What?" I tap my hand against his knee. "You were not."

"I was," he confesses with a blush. "You stepped on to the plane and…" He blows a heavy gust of air out between his lips.

"How did you end up sitting next to me in coach?" I interrupt whatever it was he was going to say.

His finger traces a line over the seam of my jeans. "I asked the flight attendant to check if anyone was sitting next to you. She said you had the window seat, the middle seat was vacant and a woman was sitting in the aisle seat."

I never saw that woman. After I sat down in my seat I don't remember anything until Ben came up the aisle and sat down. "What woman? I never saw her."

"That's because she took my seat in first class after I offered it to her in exchange for her seat in coach when she boarded the plane."

"I thought that broke some rule or something." I tilt my head towards him. "Don't you have to stay in the seat assigned to you in case something happens?"

"The flight attendant called the gate. They made a note of the change and I took the seat in coach that was beside you."

"Why?" I glance at him with a grin. "Why would you do that?"

"You have the most beautiful face I've ever seen." His finger jumps to my chin. "When I saw you walk past me, I knew I had to know you."

Chapter 10

"Ah, Kayla." His hands run down the bare skin of my back. "Please. I need to. Please."

I push my wetness into his crotch. "Just hold me like this."

"Yes," he whispers the word into my neck. "I'll hold you like this forever."

I want that. I'd kissed him after he told me he arranged to sit next to me on the airplane. It wasn't because the gesture demanded a reward. It was because I saw within him the same need that I felt that night. When I'd first looked at his face as the flight attendants ran through the finer details of what to do in case of an emergency, my eyes had locked with his. There was a mirrored reflection in his face of my want and desire. We both knew, before either of us said the cursory and expected hello, that we'd be sharing our bodies.

"Your body is perfect." His lips graze over my chin. "Do you know how perfect it is?"

He's sitting against the thick wooden headboard of his bed, his back pushing it into it, while I straddle his lap. My breasts are splayed against his chest. My hands cup his cheeks. "I like that you think it's perfect."

"Everything about you is."

I push my lips into his, running the edge of my tongue along the lush full lines of his mouth. He groans slightly, his arms tightening on my back, one hand racing down to cup my ass cheek, pulling my core over his swollen erection.

"I've missed this," I whisper into his mouth. "I've missed you."

He pulls back just enough that his lips hover next to mine as he speaks. "Tell me you trust me, Kayla. I can't do this if you don't trust me."

"I..." I edge forward wanting to feel his kiss again.

"Kayla." His hands bolt to my face. "I have so many things to tell you. I can't fuck you if you doubt me. I feel too much when I fuck you."

The growl that comes out of him with the words only arouses me more. "I want you to fuck me, Ben."

"Jesus, please." His thumb runs a path over my bottom lip. "I want to taste you. I've been craving you for days. Tell me this is okay."

"I want it." I push my breasts into his chest, pressing my core into his hard cock. "I want you so much."

"Fuck." His hands are back on my body, pushing me down. "I have to lick you."

I throw my legs open not caring that I'm on total display. He moves his tall frame with a single glide until his hands are on my ass and his head is resting against my thigh.

"Ben." I weave my hand through his hair. "Please."

He runs his finger over the lips of my slick sex. "Your cunt is so beautiful."

I push my hips back into the bed and arch my back. "I'm so close already. Do it, Ben. Please."

"You want me to lick this." His tongue spears hot over my swollen clit. "You want that, don't you?"

It's pure torture. I've never been with a man who knew exactly how to push me to the very edge of my desire with such a gentle touch. I pull on his hair, trying to guide his head back to my core. "I want it," I purr. "Do it."

"After you come on my face, I'm going to fuck you." He traces the tip of his tongue over my folds. "I'm going to fuck you so hard."

My hands jump to the bed linens, bunching the sheets in my fists. "I have to come."

"You will." He blows a puff of air over my flesh. "You're going to come for me now."

I scream out in pleasure as he scoops my ass into his hands, and dives into my pussy. His tongue expertly pulls at my clit, tracing a circle of pressure around it. I come quickly and hard. My hips buck beneath him but he doesn't stop. He only eats me harder, moaning into my flesh as I grind myself into his face.

His name falls from my lips over and over again as I ride the crest of pleasure into a deep orgasm. I cling to his head, pulling hard on his hair as he licks me softly until I finally rest my back into the bed again.

"Kayla." His lips are fluttering over mine now, the taste of my own desire mixed with his breath. "I feel so much."

I open my eyes slowly. His face is close to mine. I can sense his arms on either side of me, his hands holding up the weight of his body as they push into the bed. I stare into his face. "Ben," I whisper back.

"I would never hurt you." A tear falls from his face onto my chin. "Tell me you know I wouldn't hurt you."

"I know." I cup his cheek in my hand.

He turns his head towards my hand, pushing the gruff edge of his beard into my palm. "I kept him from you because I wanted you. You loved him for so long. I didn't want to give you back to him."

I feel all of my own emotions crashing to the surface. "I wouldn't have gone back to him."

"I lied to him to keep you." He sobs into my hand. "I lied to Parker to keep you two apart."

Chapter 11

"I followed you a few times." His hands pull my body into his chest. He's behind me now. The dusk of the evening has taken over the city and his bedroom. The only light illuminating us is the faint lights from the buildings surrounding his.

"You saw me with Noah." I trace my fingernails over my bottom lip. "I heard that when you told Parker."

"I felt empty inside when my mother died." His breath is on my bare shoulder. "It took me years to forget how brutal the pain of losing her was."

I rub my brow. "I know, Ben."

"I felt it again." He exhales audibly. "I felt it when Parker told me he loved you."

I should turn over and face him but I know that I can't keep myself together if I do that. I'd almost fallen apart when he told me he had lied to Parker to keep us apart. It didn't really matter in the big picture of my life. I knew I'd never get back together with Parker once I met Ben, but still, hearing him tell me that he'd consciously manipulated the situation, it jarred me in ways I didn't expect.

"I didn't follow you because of Noah." He runs his hand over my hair, pulling it behind my back. "I followed you because Parker kept telling me he was coming back here to see you."

"What?" I lurch forward. "Parker told you that?"

His hands guide me back into his embrace. "He'd send me messages about how lonely he was and that he wanted you back and he was getting on the next train. Then he wouldn't respond to me for hours."

I'd read those messages on his phone but I hadn't thought much of them. Whether or not Parker tried to contact me the last few weeks didn't matter anymore. It likely wouldn't have mattered then either. I was so into Ben. I was so immersed in helping him and Noah that Parker was the last thing on my mind. "So you followed me because you thought I was going to see him?"

"It's stupid," he says the words in barely more than a whisper. "It happened twice and both times just as I was walking up the street to your place, I saw you leaving. I walked behind you and when I saw you meet up with Noah, I'd leave. I was so grateful Parker wasn't in New York trying to get you back."

"You should have stopped me. You should have just talked to me, Ben."

"I wasn't rational." He leans his head into mine. "I was fighting with myself, Kayla. The selfish part of me wanted to keep you away from Parker and the part that cares for you wanted you to have the life you wanted, even if it was with him. I was terrified of making another mistake that would cost me someone important to me."

"I wish you would have told me then that you knew him," I offer quietly. I do wish for that. Regardless of whether Parker was bad for me or not, Ben took on the task of weaving a new path for my life on his own.

"History is a powerful thing." His legs move slightly. "I asked you about him weeks ago. You told me he was your first love."

I cringe at the reminder. If life offered a redo of memorable moments that you carry with you forever, that would be mine. I did love Parker back when my innocent need to have a love that lasted a lifetime clouded all my better judgment. Parker was always looking over my shoulder for the next best thing which typically came dressed in a short skirt and had blonde hair and big tits. I never measured up to his ideal. I was the plain, skinny, brunette who was always sitting in wait for him every time he decided to sow his oats. Youth may offer many things, but in my case, my teenage years offered nothing but difficult memories of poor choices.

"I fell in love with Parker the same day I got my driver's license." I pull his hands tighter around my body. "That should tell you something about how immature I was."

He laughs so loud it bounces against the walls and fills the room. It's a beautiful laugh. One I've rarely heard. "You were young. People don't think straight when they're young."

"I'm still too young to think straight." I reach back to run my palm over his hip. "I'm not too young to know Parker is bad for me."

"When I first knew you two had been together, we were struggling with the Noah stuff." He adjusts his body slightly, pushing his knee over my legs. "I was worried."

"About what?" My hand slides down to caress the skin of his thigh.

"That Noah would tell you about what happened with our mother and you'd run back to Parker if you knew he wanted you."

It fits. Ben was almost frantic at times before I learned of the circumstances surrounding his mother's death. "I didn't run away when I found out, Ben."

"That only made me want you so much more." His lips push into my shoulder. "You were so kind and good to me. You listened to me talk about her and Noah. You didn't give up on me."

"I wouldn't have given up on you." I mean it. The thought of walking away from Ben when he was trying to claw his way out of that emotional hell that was created after his mother died, wasn't something I ever could have done. I cared too much about him.

"I thought you had when I saw you in Parker's apartment." His breath hitches before he continues, "I thought you were moving back in with him."

"What?" I flip over so quickly he can't react. "You didn't really think that."

"I went to Boston to meet with some doctors for a project I'm working on." He stops to push a few hairs away from my forehead and out of my eyes. "I got a call from Parker saying he wanted to talk to you to tell you he loved you. I wasn't in New York. I felt so far away from you."

"You had no idea I was in Boston," I offer sullenly. He couldn't have known. I went there to surprise him with the news that Noah was ready to let him back into his life.

He shakes his head briefly. "I panicked. I imagined Parker calling you and everything changing that day."

"So you went to talk to him?"

He leans forward brushing his lips softly across mine. "I asked for his address. I wanted to do it in person so I could control things."

"You told him he could have me back once you got Noah back." I don't say it with malice or anger. I say it because it's what I heard.

"Kayla." He runs his hand along my jawline. "I would never have let him have you."

"I heard you say it." It's been the one part of that day that has haunted me relentlessly. Hearing Ben essentially tell Parker that I was his to have back was unforgettable. It made me feel like a pair of old borrowed shoes that no longer serve their purpose so they're sent back to their owner, weathered and torn.

"I met Parker in the lobby of his building." His grip on me tightens. "The very first thing he said to me was that he bought a train ticket for New York. He was taking the ring he bought and coming to see you."

I hadn't thought there was anything to their conversation beyond what I heard when I was standing in the bedroom after they walked into the apartment. "I didn't know that."

"We were down there for more than ten minutes. I tried to convince him over and over again not to leave Boston."

I wish I would have heard that exchange. It would have offered a lot more insight than the fragmented part of their conversation I heard. "It doesn't change what I heard."

"I was grasping at straws at that point." His body stiffens. "I'd told him in the lobby that I needed more time with you. I told him it was because of Noah. I was worried that if I told him I was involved with you as more than friends that he'd beat a path straight to your door and tell you that I knew him."

"So what I heard when you two walked in was…"

"It was my desperate attempt to get Parker to stay put in Boston so I'd have time to confess everything to you and beg you not to leave me for him," he interrupts me in a rush.

I can't look in him in the eyes as I process it all. The words I heard him say to Parker that day had bitten right through me. They'd stolen all the promise I felt for a future with him away in a flash. "You didn't seem very surprised to see me there."

He tilts his head back as his jaw clenches. "I was in shock. I thought that was it. I thought you'd made up your mind and that you were there to take him back."

I shudder physically at the thought. "You were so calm and you just left me there with him."

"When I saw you two together, it finally hit me." He pushes his hand into his chest. "I saw how real the pain was for you. I saw how hurt you were by both of us. I knew I had to leave you there to find your way out of it."

I should feel abandoned by that. I should feel as though Ben ran away to leave me in a cage of uncertainty with Parker, but that's not what I feel at all. "You left me there to make my own choice."

"I did." He closes his eyes briefly. "It's the hardest thing I've ever done. I knew I had to stop manipulating it all. I knew that if I lost you, that it was because it was what you needed to be happy."

Chapter 12

"I have to go." He pulls his boxer briefs on before he stumbles against the bed in his haste to get his pants back on. "Shit, Kayla. I'm sorry."

I nod. I'd watched all the color drain from his face when he answered his cell not more than two minutes ago. He'd barely responded after listening to whatever the person calling said to him. "Is it work?"

"No." He reaches over the bed to pull his shirt from where it landed when he'd stripped his clothes off after tenderly undressing me. "It's just…"

"Ben?" I'm on my knees on the bed now, the sheet lazily wrapped around my nude body. "What is it? Is it Noah or Ron?"

His eyes scan my face. "Get dressed. I need you."

I don't hesitate at all as I jump to my feet to pull my jeans and sweater back on. I push my feet into my flats quickly and before I have time to run my hand through my hair, I'm chasing him through the bedroom door.

"I need my bag." He pushes his cell phone into my palm. "Hold this for me."

I reach for the phone, tossing it into my purse as I watch him fling open the door to a closet. He rummages through it quickly, pulling out a black overnight bag. "We need to find a cab now."

He's out the apartment door before I have time to ask any questions. My eyes settle on his keys. They're still sitting atop the desk where he threw them when we first arrived hours earlier. I snatch them into my fist as I race out the door, locking it behind me before I dart into the waiting elevator.

He holds out his hand. "I'm sorry."

"For what?" I push myself up to my tiptoes to graze my lips across his cheek.

"I need you so much." His hand rests on my back, nudging me closer as he settles his lips against my hair. "I really need you."

He scoops my hand into his as the elevator chimes its arrival in the lobby. I can barely keep up to his wide strides. We breeze past the doorman who takes one look at Ben before he's on the curb, whistling for a cab. He knows. The doorman has seen him like this before.

I don't say a word as Ben pushes me into the backseat of the taxi with a knowing nod to the doorman who leans in the passenger side window to give the driver an address I don't recognize. I hold tightly to Ben's hand as his legs shake and he slaps his other hand against the seat next to him.

"If you avoided the park altogether, we'd get there faster."

The driver doesn't acknowledge the words but judging by the quick and unexpected right turn the car takes, he gets the message loud and clear. The taxi races through the crowded streets as we sit in utter silence.

"Pay him, Kayla. Please, pay him." Ben pulls his wallet from the pocket of his pants as he opens the car door when we finally come to a screeching halt. "Meet me inside."

I pull a few bills from the wallet as I watch Ben sprint through the doors of a dark building on a tree lined street. I hand the money to the driver telling him to keep the change. I reach behind me to grab my purse. My heart is racing. Ben's disappeared inside the entrance to the building and I have no idea what awaits me when I follow him in. The only thing I do know is that I have no choice.

***

The moment I pull open the curtained glass front door I know what I'm stepping into it. Children's voices pierce through all the other noise in the building. Two youngsters race past me at break neck speed. A woman nods in my direction from where she's perched on a wooden rocking chair, an infant nestled tightly in a blanket in her arms. The faint purple hue of a lingering bruise covers the entire left side of her face.

"I'm looking for Dr. Foster," I say to her because beyond this point I have no idea which direction I need to take to find Ben.

"Dr. Ben?" A little boy with brown hair and blue eyes pops up in front of me. "I can take you to Dr. Ben."

I accept the tender, unspoken, invitation to grab his tiny hand in mine. He pulls his feet along the tile floor to a room in the corner. "Dr. Ben is in there."

The faint sound of crying greets me as I push the wooden door open. I see him. Ben's next to a stretcher where a teenage boy is resting. He's talking to a woman in Spanish. Even though I can't comprehend the words, I can hear the comfort in them. He's consoling her. She's nodding fiercely as she stares down at the child.

"Kayla." He turns when he hears the creek of the old door as I shut it. "Come."

I walk slowly to where he's standing. "I've called for an ambulance. I'm taking Peter to the hospital."

I glance down at the boy. He's awake but his face is awash with pain. He's hooked up to an IV. Ben's bag sits atop the foot of the bed. "What's wrong?" I ask, not because I'll have any grasp of the details Ben will offer, but because I can see the sheer fear in the boy's face and in the face of his mother who is clinging tightly to Ben's hand.

"It's his appendix. It needs to be removed." He taps his hand against my thigh. "I'm ride in the ambulance with him. Can you bring his mother to the hospital in a cab?"

I nod. "Your hospital?"

His eyes dart to the mother before they settle back on my face. "No. There's a community hospital a few blocks from here. We're taking him there."

The boy raises his hand to get Ben's attention and he turns towards him. I watch in silence as he speaks to the boy in Spanish, his hand caressing the young man's forehead.

Chapter 13

I can't distinguish much of what transpired between Ben and the doctor in the ER at the community hospital we just arrived at. I'd hailed a taxi as they were loading Peter into the ambulance and the driver saw the thrill in a good chase so we were on the ambulance's bumper almost the entire way here. The emergency room in this place is swelling beyond its capacity. If it's even possible, it's busier than the hospital where Ben works.

I'll never understand medical jargon and as Ben explains in Spanish what is happening to Peter's mother I stand to the side watching him trying to calm her down.

"Dr. Foster?" A woman carrying a clipboard approaches all of us from the left. "We need to talk."

He glances down at Peter's mother. His hand flies through the air towards the waiting room as he says something quickly to her. She nods in response and turns on her heel in search of a chair in the over cramped, obviously, under-funded small space.

"What is it?" He turns back towards the woman with the clipboard.

"Insurance?" She cocks a brow and dots the tip of the pencil in her hand against her tongue. "I need that for the patient you just brought in."

"No." It's curt and direct.

"No?" She parrots back. "He doesn't have any?"

"Where is Melody?" He looks past her to the reception desk where several women are trying to quell the growing line of people waiting to see a doctor. "I usually deal with Melody."

"She's left for the day." She taps her foot against the tile floor. "You need to deal with me today."

He turns towards me without notice. "Kayla, I need my wallet."

I reach into my purse and pull it out, handing it to him without question.

He opens the billfold and yanks free a credit card. "This will take care of it."

"You're paying for his surgery?" The woman stares at the credit card. "Is this even going to cover the entire cost?"

Ben's head snaps in her direction. "Use the credit card, get me a lab coat and get out of my way."

"You don't work here." She's on his heels as he walks towards the reception desk.

He turns swiftly to face her, his expression a mixture of anxiety and frustration. "I volunteer here. Melody knows that. You'll learn it."

She doesn't say a word as he turns back towards me. He walks right past her, grabs my shoulders in his hands and leans down to kiss me gently on my mouth.

"I'll be here all night, Kayla." He whispers against my cheek. "I thought we'd be able to get back into my bed so I could finish what I started, but they need me here."

I run my fingers over his chin. "Thank you for bringing me here."

"Thank you for everything," he says softly. "Go home. Sleep. I'll call you tomorrow."

***

My eyes dart to where my phone is perched atop the pillow next to mine. I reach for it, pushing my hand against the screen to wake it from its sleep. It's just past five in the morning. I'd finally fallen asleep less than an hour ago. The adrenaline high I was feeling after watching Ben race to help that boy had stolen any chance I had to get a good night's rest. My mind and my heart have been on overdrive ever since I left the hospital.

I hear the faint knock that woke me again. This time I'm certain it's not my neighbor's door that is being assaulted, it's my own. I pull a robe around my nude body before I walk into the hall. The overhead light takes a few seconds to flicker on after I hit the switch.

"Who is it?" I call through the heavy wooden door. It's not the first time this has happened. It's actually the third. A trio of middle-aged frat boy wannabes lives in the apartment above mine. Late night pizza and beer deliveries seem to be the bane of their existence. If I can get rid of the delivery person without having to open my door to subject them to the horror of my messy bed hair, my day will start on the right foot.

"Dr. Foster." His voice calls through the silence. "I'm making a house call."

I unhinge the dual locks that keep me somewhat safe from the outside world. I swing the door open quickly and pull him inside.

His lips are on mine in an instant. His kiss is a sweet mixture of peppermint gum and coffee. "You stole my keys."

I laugh into his mouth. "You gave them to me."

It hadn't even crossed my mind to fish Ben's keys from my purse before he kissed me goodbye on the curb in front of the hospital after hailing me a taxi. I'd like to think that it was my subconscious mind wanting to hold onto more of him, but it was so late and I was beyond tired.

"You came all this way to get them?" I lean into his body, relishing in the feel of his strong arms around me.

"No. I came here to fuck you. I'll need those keys back though, although…"

I stop him with a kiss. I didn't get past the point where he said he wanted to fuck me. My sex had been aching since last night when he brought me to the edge with his mouth. We hadn't made love before the entire night shifted into a rescue mission.

"Keep the keys." He pulls back far enough that the words linger on my cheek. "I want you to have the keys."

"No." I shake my head against his. "Not yet."

"They're just keys, Kayla." His hands are on my robe, pulling it open. "You can hide them in the bottom of your purse or a drawer here. I just want you to have them."

I work on the buttons on his dress shirt. "Do you want a key to my place?"

"I want your wet cunt around my cock." His hands drop to his pants, undoing the belt and zipper quickly. "It's been so long since I've been inside of you."

"The bedroom," I whisper into his neck. "Take me to my bedroom."

He scoops me up in one easy, graceful movement as his lush lips take over my mouth.

Chapter 14

"Stop moving." He pushes against my mound with his hand. "Kayla, Christ, just stop."

I arch my back up, pulling my chest away from his. I'd ridden his beautiful, thick sheathed cock to an orgasm already. Now, I'm sitting atop his trembling body, feeling him pulse within me. "I want you to come."

"No." He drops his cheek into the sheet. "I want to feel this. I just want you to stay like this so I can be inside of you."

I push back slightly so I can feel the pressure of his crotch against my clit. "It's so good, Ben. Please just let me fuck you."

"You need to stop talking." He laughs aloud. "Seriously, your voice is ridiculously hot when you say things like that."

"Things like what?" I clench myself around the thick root drawing out a loud, slow moan from deep within him.

"Fuck, please." His hands leap to my thighs. "You're so vocal when I'm fucking you. I love it."

"You love when I say how much I like your cock inside of me." I push back so I can trace my index finger over my clit. "You want to hear me tell you how wet I get when I know you're going to fuck me."

He stares at my hand, watching me trace lazy circles over my own desire. "I want to watch you get yourself off. I want to watch you finger your beautiful cunt."

I moan from the pure shamelessness of his words. "You want me to do that now?"

He pushes me back slightly. A small rush of air escapes him as his cock slides out of my body.

"Ben, no," I whimper. "I want it inside of me."

"Touch yourself," he commands as his large hand circles his cock. "Touch it and show me."

I lean back and pull my right hand through my folds. I stare at his cock, my body still feeling bereft from the loss of its thickness and length. I moan from the sight of his hand around it, stroking it slowly.

"You're so beautiful, Kayla," he growls the words. "You're so fucking beautiful."

I lean back farther and close my eyes, losing myself in not only the feeling of the approaching orgasm but the sound of his deep, sweet voice. "I'm close," I whisper into the air. "I'm so close, Ben."

"Let me see you come." His hand covers my own. "Open your eyes. I love your eyes."

I look at him under the cast of heavy lids. I call out his name as I dive into the depth of my desire.

"Fuck," he says softly. "God. You're so amazing."

I rest my hands on his muscular chest as I come down from the high. My hair is a matted mess on my shoulders. The mist of perspiration he's pulled from me resting against my skin.

"I need you." His voice is low and deep as he pulls me closer to him and in one easy movement flips us over.

He enters me swiftly and hard. I cry out from the bite of flashing pain. He's so deep. I'm so tender from coming already but my hips don't betray my body's lustful need for him. I push my feet into the bed and push up to match his every stroke as he takes my body again.

"Fuck, fuck, Kayla, fuck," he spits out the words in a quick progression as his body rushes towards its own release.

***

"I have to go to the hospital." He buttons up the same wrinkled shirt he's been wearing since I first saw him outside his building yesterday afternoon.

"Which one?" I look at his reflection in the mirror behind me. I'm just freshly showered. The invitation I'd offered him to join me had been interrupted by his phone. He answered it quickly, speaking in Spanish.

"The one I work at during the day." He leans forward to kiss my shoulder. "I have a split shift there today."

"You haven't slept, Ben." I turn around to kiss his mouth. "You can't do this to yourself."

"I'm very good at functioning with little sleep." His eyes wander over my nude body. "You have to agree."

I blush from the reminder of what we just did in my bed. It's not out of embarrassment. I love sharing my body with him. It's out of desire. I've never come more than once when I've been with a man before. Ben can draw more pleasure from my body in thirty minutes than I knew was even possible.

"I still owe you an entire day in my bed." He takes the towel I'm holding from me and carefully blots it against my hair. "We can plan that when you have a day off."

I sigh at the gentle reminder that I have an actual job I need to get to. "I wish I could change jobs."

"You can." He reaches to pick up my hairbrush from the counter. "You don't like your job?"

"It's so boring," I giggle at the understatement. I've been close to falling asleep most days lately. Vivian's incessant need to get me to take care of her personal tasks has resulted in my organizing her family pictures onto flash drives. It may be interesting if every person she's related do didn't bear an overwhelming resemblance to her.

He carefully runs the brush through my hair, stopping whenever he reaches a knot. "Why don't you look for something else?"

"They'll pay for my master's degree," I begin. "I mean they'll cover part of my tuition which would be a big help."

"I can pay for that." He doesn't hesitate as he makes the offer.

"No." I stall his hand with my own. "I won't take money from you."

"You can work it off." He wraps his arms around my shoulders. "Or it can be a loan if you want."

I don't want to ever be financially dependent on a man. I was that way when I first moved back to Boston to live with Parker. I'd actually taken a job at Star Bistro then, a college coffee shop, so I could make enough money to buy my own things. That was one of the reasons I still hoped to get the damage deposit from the old apartment back at some point. My savings account balance was nothing to celebrate.

"I'll figure it out." I smile tenderly at him in the mirror. He really is the most generous person I've ever met. Watching him hand his credit card to the woman at the hospital last night had only punctuated that fact in my mind. It goes beyond money though. His desperate need to get to that homeless shelter to save that boy's life and his willingness to volunteer at a hospital because they are understaffed is the core of who he is.

"I know you will. You're the smartest woman I know."

Chapter 15

"We haven't talked about the wedding much lately." Alexa breathes a sigh as she runs her manicured fingernail over the edge of the coffee cup.

I've been neglecting her since I left for Boston. She hasn't complained. In fact, she's been nothing but gracious and kind with endless text messages and phone calls asking me if there's anything she can do to help me. She also hasn't pried when it's come to my relationship with Ben. I know she's dying to know where we stand and if I'm being utterly honest with myself, I'm bursting at the seams to share things with her. "I'm sorry about that, Lex."

"You have a lot going on." She taps her hand over mine. "Tell me what's happening in your life."

I start with the boring bits about work and waiting to hear on whether I've been accepted into the master's program. I don't delve into the details about how I'm completely unfulfilled working for Vivian. In the grand scheme of things, I have a job that pays well, offers me great benefits and allows me the opportunity to get an education I'd otherwise never be able to afford.

We pause when her phone rings. She pulls her finger over the screen and immediately starts telling Sadie everything she needs done between this very moment in time and her big day. I stare at her, watching how animated her expression is as she talks about the final alterations on her dress.

"I'm sorry, Kayla." She finally puts the phone back on the table just as I finish the last sip of my now cold coffee. "Sadie is a bundle of nerves."

"That makes two of you," I say with a grin while holding up my thumb and index finger. "If I get married one day, remind me to elope."

"If Ben is anything like Noah, he'll want a big wedding."

I don't respond. I can't because it would mean I'd be acknowledging something that I haven't even allowed myself to fantasize about. Ben and I are still testing the very shallow waters of our relationship. We haven't even gotten past everything that happened in Boston a few weeks ago. It still hurts to think about the words he said to Parker. He may have been saying them to hold onto me but my doubt hasn't completely disappeared yet.

"Has Noah spent any time with Ben?" I ask to buck us off the uncomfortable saddle she's put us in. I won't talk about anyone's marriage but Alexa's. That's a hard and fast rule I'm definitely sticking to.

"They're having lunch together today." She shrugs her left shoulder. "Noah seemed stoked about it."

"Ben didn't mention it." It stings to say the words even though it's juvenile to be hurt by something so mundane. I hadn't mentioned that I'd be seeing Alexa to Ben either when he kissed me goodbye after spending the night at my place.

"Do you trust him?"

I wish I could say I'm surprised by the question. I'm not. Even though Lex sang all of Ben's praises after I came back from Boston, I know that she's still reserving final judgment on him. I can tell that she sees Ben as the lesser of two evils in her mind's competition of him and Parker.

"Is there a reason I shouldn't?" I push it back on her because I don't want to lie to her. If I was forced to answer her question, I'd have to tell her that there's still a fraction of doubt within my heart.

"I don't know of any reason you shouldn't trust Ben." She tips her chin in my direction as she throws me a wink. "I'm taking cues from Noah anyways."

"What does that mean?"

"You know he thinks of you as a younger sister, right?"

"He said that to you?" My voice rises as I ask the question.

She raises both brows. "Noah wants only the best for you. He told me you're his favorite."

"His favorite what?" I ask tentatively. I'm almost afraid of what the answer will be.

"You're his favorite of my friends."

"You mean he likes me more than he likes Sadie?" I raise my hand. "One point for Kayla. Finally."

"Don't tell Sadie."

"Why? Because she'll fall to pieces?" I smirk. "I'll keep it quiet. It's our little secret."

"I'm being serious." She runs her finger along the edge of her cell phone's case. "He went to so much trouble to make sure you weren't making a mistake."

I'm lost. If she's referring to the infrequent meetings I had with Noah to discuss Ben, that doesn't seem like that much trouble to me. "I'm not sure what you mean."

"That file of stuff, he has." She pulls her index finger and thumb apart about an inch. "That file is huge. It didn't come cheap."

I scratch the back of my head. "What are you talking about?"

"The private investigator," she whispers the words so softly I wonder if she thinks we're being watched by one right now. "That man he hired to get the goods on Ben."

"Get the goods?" Apparently hiring a private investigator constitutes the need to use their distinctive lingo. "What?"

"Shit." She scrolls her finger over her phone. "I should call Noah. Shit."

"Lex." I reach across the table to pull her phone from her grasp. "You've already said a lot. Please just tell me what the hell is going on."

Her eyes scan my face. "Noah was worried about you. He wasn't sure of Ben."

It's a start but none of this is news to me at all. "What did he do? He hired a private investigator?"

"The guy did an extensive background check on Ben. There's financials in there, employment stuff, everything."

It's intrusive. "Why would he do that?"

"It was for you." She points her index finger at my hand. "He did it to make sure Ben was good enough for you."

Chapter 16

There's that saying about being stuck between a rock and a hard place and it's never made any sense to me until this moment. Let's say that Noah is the rock and Ben is the hard place. I'm staring into his face right now and the good part of me wants to tell him that Noah has his entire life summarized in a reasonably thick manila folder. The other part of me, that's the part that wants things to stay the way they are right now, is telling me that there's no harm in it. Noah is just taking care of me, which is touching in a way that would be sentimental if it wasn't so inappropriate.

"Spit it out, Kayla." He runs his lips across my forehead.

"I swallowed it all after you came," I say into his chest.

I feel the laugher roll through his strong frame. He pulls me even closer. "You're everything I'm ever going to need in my life."

"I saw Alexa yesterday." I'm siding on the hard place. "We talked about you."

"I saw Noah," he whispers the words into my hair. "We talked about you."

I know. I need to bite the curiosity I'm feeling in the ass and not ask what they were discussing. I have to. I need to just tell Ben that Noah investigated him. He deserves to know that his brother knows everything about him. I'd want to know if someone pulled up that much sensitive information on me.

"What did you say about me?"

Who am I kidding? I'm not going to be able to think straight until I find out what they talked about.

"Noah told me you're a good friend to him," he says without any reservation. "He told me he likes hanging out with you."

"He told me that too," I offer back. That resulted in a net gain of exactly zero. "Is that all he said?"

"Why?" I can hear the amusement in his voice. "Maybe we talked about private things."

I lurch up off his chest so I'm facing him directly. I arch a brow. "Private things?" I try not to crack a wide grin. "You two weren't even on speaking terms a few weeks ago. I highly doubt you talk about private things."

"We're brothers." He traces his finger along my brow. "Actually, we're twins. We share a lot of private things."

He's not smiling. This has moved effortlessly from teasing into something more serious. "How are things between you two?"

"New." He darts his tongue over his bottom lip. "We're still working on figuring things out but no one was punched during lunch so we're off to a good start."

Ben and I have never discussed what happened in Noah's hospital room the night he was stabbed. He knows that I know. He has to know that Noah shared a great deal about their broken connection with me during all the time we spent together. "Do you feel good about things between you?"

"I feel really good about things between my brother and me."

It's there again. I don't think about it as much as I did when it was fresh and pressing against every part of my heart. It's the last bit of doubt that has held onto me and now is the point in time when I can finally let it go. "You're not going to leave me now that you and Noah are working on things, are you?"

His breathing stops as his hands reach to cup my cheeks. "I will never leave you. There is nothing in this world that can take you away from me. If you didn't want me anymore, you have to be the one doing the breaking up. I'm here to stay."

"I don't want that," I whisper into his mouth. "I want you to stay."

***

"If I told you I love you would you say it back to me?" He's standing in the doorway, his hands resting above his head against the wooden doorframe. I can see the outline of his muscular frame. He's shirtless. He's only wearing sweat pants and nothing else.

I pull my hand to cover my mouth. "Not yet. I need to tell you something first."

He doesn't move from where he's standing. I can't make out his face. The room is too dark. "What is it, Kayla?"

"Come closer." I pat my hand against the mattress. I'd fallen asleep in his arms after we'd talked. It's hours later now and the ringing of his cell phone had woken us both. "Is everything okay? I heard your phone ringing."

"It was Peter's mother." He lowers himself next to me, bending his knee so he's facing me directly. "He's running a very low fever. It's nothing. I told her to keep him in bed and well hydrated. I'll drop by their house early tomorrow morning with another round of antibiotics. I told her to call me if he gets worse before then."

"Do you do that a lot?" It's something I've wanted to ask about since I watched him hand his credit card over to pay for Peter's surgery.

He doesn't make eye contact with me. "Do I do what a lot?"

"Pay for people's surgeries and medicine?"

"I do it when I need to." He slides his eyes over my face. "I take people from the shelter to that hospital sometimes. I usually talk to an administrator named Melody. I volunteer there and she gives me a break on the cost of things."

"You're really generous." I reach to touch his hand. "I've never known anyone as generous as you."

"My mother was really generous." He smiles at me. "She'd give anything to any person who needed it. She taught me that life is about giving."

"Noah missed that lesson," I tease.

"Noah gives in his own way," he counters. "He's been through a lot in his life. He's had a lot to deal with."

There are the generous parts of him shining through again. "You see the best in him."

"When we were five," he begins before he scoops my hand into his. "On our fifth birthday our parents gave us bicycles."

I smile at the thought of Ben and Noah as children. I've never even seen an image of either of them as youngsters. It's a very hard picture to conjure in my mind's eyes. "Did you learn to ride them together?"

"No." He chuckles softly. "Noah got on that thing and took off. It was like he was born to ride a two wheeler. He rode circles around me."

"Competition is part of being a sibling." I've had to deal with that my entire life with my own brother. "It's not necessarily a bad thing."

"It's a really healthy thing." His tongue darts over his bottom lip. "I tried for days to get it. I couldn't keep my balance. My dad gave up trying to teach me."

We don't discuss Ron much, but I know it eats at Ben that he's never got the same approval and affection from his father that Noah has. "Are you confessing to me that you can't ride a bike?" I want to lighten the mood before I tell Ben about Noah and the private investigator. I want utter honesty in our relationship. I need it after what we've been through.

"Noah taught me." His voice cracks. "He held on to the back of my bike and tried so hard to balance it with me on it."

"That's why he's the one with all the muscles?"

"Hey." He pulls up his arm, bending it to show off his impressive bicep. "I'm ripped too."

I laugh at the playful expression on his face.

"It took months but Noah helped me learn how to balance on that bike." He squeezes my hand. "He never gave up on me."

Chapter 17

"I don't like secrets, Ben."

We're under the covers now. I can hear him breathing peacefully. His hand is moving slowly up and down my hip.

"I don't want secrets between us."

I scratch my nose. My stomach is flopping around so heavily within my body that I'm surprised he can't feel it against his side. "I know something about Noah that I think you should know. It may not matter, but it's your right to know it."

"Is it something Noah told you about me?" He doesn't move. "I know Noah has talked about me to you. You know most of what happened between us."

I nod against his chest. I should pull myself up so I'm looking right at him when I say this. "Alexa actually told me something yesterday."

"What did she tell you?" His hand is on my chin now, running along my jawbone.

I adjust myself, grabbing his hand with my own. I bring it to my lips and hold it against them. I need to be as close to him as possible. "She told me Noah did something to protect me."

"Whatever that it is, I'm grateful to him for that."

I smile up at him. "Noah wants the best for me."

"I'm the best for you," he says quickly. "I know that I am. That's why I want to tell you how I feel."

I pull his hand closer to my lips again. "Let me say this first."

His brow jumps up. "Say it, Kayla."

"Alexa told me that Noah hired a private investigator to look at your life when he knew that we were getting close."

His lips part slightly as if he's going to say something. It's in that moment that I feel him pull away. He yanks his hand free of mine, before he slides his body out from under the sheet.

"Ben?" I call after him as he walks quickly out of the room. I hear his footsteps along the hardwood floor and then there's nothing but total silence.

I turn over. I feel the panic before it hits my body. I'm nauseous. I threw that at him without any warning at all. He was just starting to feel close to Noah again and I tossed it at him like a live hand grenade. I should have gone to Noah. I should have fucking gone to Noah and confronted him about this so he could tell Ben himself.

I reach down in the darkness looking for Ben's robe. I saw it on the chair near the window earlier. It's here. I know it is. I have to stop and catch my breath.

"Kayla?" His voice is behind me. "Kayla, turn around."

I do just as his hand touches the light switch. The sudden brilliant light that floods the bedroom blinds me momentarily and I cover my eyes with my hands. "It's too bright, Ben."

"I'm sorry." I hear movement behind me. "I'll dim the light."

I heave a sigh of relief as I slide my hands into my lap. I'm still not facing him. "I didn't mean to just throw that at you. I know it must make you feel violated. I would feel that way if..."

I hear his heavy footsteps coming closer. Then I see his legs. He's holding something. "Noah gave me this yesterday."

I look at his hands. He's holding a manila folder overflowing with papers.

"Noah told me about it. He gave it all to me to destroy." He hands it to me. "You can read it if you want."

I stare at it. It's Ben's entire life all in one place. Every bank transaction he's ever made, every job he's ever held, and all the places he's lived are documented in the papers falling out of the folder.

"He gave you this?"

He swallows hard before he sits next to me. "I have nothing to hide. If doing this helped Noah trust me again, I'm glad he did it. If reading it helps you in any way, I want you to do that."

"You're not angry?" There's more excitement in my tone than surprise. "How can you not be angry?"

"I would do anything to show my brother that I'm a good, honest, decent man." He taps his fingers against his leg. "I would do anything and everything in my power to show you that I'm a good, honest, decent man."

"I know that you are," I say it with no reservation at all. "I don't need to read anything here to know that."

"I want you to read one thing." He pulls the file into his own lap and thumbs through some of the documents. "This is what I want you to read."

I take the piece of paper from him and hold it in front of me. It's a printed document of some sort. I start reading it line-by-line, stopping twice to look up at Ben. "I don't understand what it is."

"I live a simple life." He closes his eyes briefly as if to gather his thoughts. "My mother left me an enormous amount of money. I will never use that money in my lifetime. I already have everything I could possibly need."

I stare at the paper he handed to me. "Are you funding this yourself?"

"I was." His hand runs over the back of my hair. "Noah is funding half of it now with his inheritance. He insisted on it when I saw him yesterday."

"The Foster Foundation," I whisper the words softly as I run my hand over where they are printed at the top of the paper. "You're doing this to help children."

"Children." He points to the paper. "Women, men, anyone who needs medical care and can't afford it."

"You're doing this for your mother?"

"I want to do good things for her. I want her to be proud of who I am today."

I watch as a tear falls from my cheek and onto the paper. "I'm sorry," I mutter as I wipe my hand across the document.

"You didn't read the last line, Kayla." He traces a path over the bottom of the paper with his finger. "Read that to me."

I hold the paper in front of me, trying to decipher the letters through my tears. "It says, director of operations..." I stall to pull my hand over my mouth. "Director of operations is Kayla Monroe."

"It's your job if you want it."

"When did you set this up?" I dart my eyes over the document looking for a date.

He pulls me closer to his side. "I've been meeting colleagues in Boston for months to get the wheels in motion. I was there when you and I met and again when I saw you at... at your old apartment," he stammers. "I had talked about you as a potential candidate for the job that Saturday morning, less than an hour before I saw you. You have so much to give to others and you're smart."

"You trust me to run a foundation in your mother's honor?" I sob through the words.

"I trust you with everything."

I reach up to cradle his cheek in my hand. "Say it now, Ben. Say it and I'll say it back."

He turns his entire body to face me. He takes the paper from my grasp and sets it on the bed as he leans in close and whispers the words I've wanted to hear since he sat down next to me on the airplane. "I love you Kayla Monroe. I really love you."

"I love you too Dr. Ben Foster. I love you."

Epilogue

1 Year Later

"Kayla, what are you doing here? Are you sick?"

I've visited Ben at the hospital enough times this past year to know that he passes by this exact spot in the hallway near the emergency room entrance at least half a dozen times an hour. If I want to talk to him while he's working, this is the place I need to be.

"I'm not sick." I push a breath out between my lips. I can already tell this is going to be much more difficult than I ever imagined. "It's not that."

"Are you already done class for the day?" His eyes dart up to the large clock hanging on the wall of the waiting room. "It's that late already?"

It's after seven. I'd worked half a day at the foundation and then went straight to class. I had wanted to postpone getting my master's degree, but Ben wouldn't hear of it. Once he got Noah and Alexa to take his side, I had little choice but to schedule my classes around my work schedule. I can't complain though. I love pursuing my own dream, knowing that I'm doing something valuable for a living. It's even more fulfilling since I'm paying my own way by using part of the salary I'm earning doing something I truly love. My work at the foundation fuels me in a way that I've never felt before. It's quickly become my passion and next to loving Ben, it's been purpose in life. It has been rather, until today.

"Are you going to come home soon?" I'm here to coax him into leaving the hospital with me. Our time isn't nearly as limited as I feared it would be. We steal moments away for each other every single day and our promise to never keep secrets has only strengthened our already unbreakable bond. I'm here now to convince him to join me for dinner, even though I doubt I'll eat much at all. I'm so nervous and nauseous.

He licks his lips as he pushes me against the wall. "Why are you so eager to get me home? Do you want me to eat your…"

"Meatloaf?" I ask loudly as an intern wheels an elderly patient in a wheelchair right past us. "We can have meatloaf tonight."

He leans forward and brushes his lush lips over mine. "I'll eat that and more the minute we're in the door."

"Can you come now?" I'm so anxious. I've never been as excited to share news with Ben as I am today. It's been a total of forty-five minutes since I found out but it feels like forty-five years.

"There's a supply closet around the corner you can blow me in." He pulls on my hand. "I can come in there now."

I swat my hand over the nametag that is hanging around his neck. "I'm not talking about sex."

"Fuck." He winks at me. "I am."

"Ben, please." I stomp my foot in jest. "I just want you to come home so I can tell you something."

"Tell me here." His eyes dart over my face. "What's wrong, Kayla?"

"Do you remember when you said..." my voice trails just as we both hear his name announced over the hospital's loudspeaker.

"Hold that thought." He grabs my shoulder. "I put in a call to a surgeon in Boston. I need to take that call in my office."

"Wait." I reach forward to grab his lab coat. "I just need a minute."

"Something isn't right." He runs his hand over my forehead. "You haven't been well. You've been sleeping more than normal. There's a virus going around. I want you to go into exam room three and wait..."

"I'm pregnant." I close my eyes tightly. "I'm...I mean... we're having a baby, Ben."

I feel movement in front of me but he doesn't say a word. This was my only fear. This is why I didn't tell him when my period was late. We haven't talked about when we'd have children yet. I don't know if he'll be as completely thrilled as I am.

"Kayla," he finally says my name in barely more than a whisper. "Open your beautiful blue eyes."

I do. I do it slowly. He's there but he's on his knees. A small ring box is resting in his palm. "I've been carrying this ring in my pocket for a week. I was going to ask you on my birthday but today, this is our real birthday."

I nod through a sob. "It's our birthday." I rub my hand over his on my still flat stomach.

"You have given me more than I've ever deserved in life, Kayla. I love you with every part of me. I will always love you." His eyes are filled with tears. "I will always love you and our baby."

"I love you too. I love you so much."

"Please be my wife. Marry me, Kayla. Marry me tomorrow."

I nod before I shake my head. "I'll marry you but not tomorrow."

He laughs as he slips the beautiful pear shaped diamond ring onto my finger. "I'll marry you on whatever day you choose and I will stay married to you until I take my last breath."

I lean down, cup his handsome face in my palms and kiss the man I love.

Thank You!

Thank you for purchasing my book. I can't even begin to put to words what it means to me. If you enjoyed it, please remember to write a review for it. Let me know your thoughts! I want to keep my readers happy.

I have more standalones and a new series in the works for you as well as updates, please visit my website, www.deborahbladon.com. There are interactive forums and other goodies to check out.

If you want to chat with me personally, please LIKE my page on Facebook. I love connecting with all of my readers because without you, none of this would be possible. www.facebook.com/authordeborahbladon

Thank you, for everything.

About the Author

Deborah Bladon has never read a romance hero she didn't like. Her love for romance novels began when she was old enough to board the bus, library card in hand to check out the newest Harlequin paperbacks. She's a Canadian by heart, and by passport, but you can often spot her in New York City sipping a latte and looking for inspiration for her next story. Manhattan is definitely her second home.

She cherishes her family and believes that each day is a gift for writing, for reading, and for loving.